THE NINETY-NINTH FLOOR

A SWALLOW EDITIONS BOOK
Founder and Series Editor: Rafik Schami

THE NINETY-NINTH FLOOR

Jana Fawaz Elhassan

translated by Michelle Hartman

Interlink Books

An imprint of Interlink Publishing Group, Inc.

Northampton, Massachusetts

First published 2017 by

INTERLINK BOOKS
An imprint of Interlink Publishing Group, Inc.
46 Crosby Street, Northampton, Massachusetts 01060
www.interlinkbooks.com

Published as part of the Swallow Editions series.
Founder and Series Editor: Rafik Schami

Library of Congress Cataloging-in-Publication Data

Names: Hasan, Janā Fawwāz author. | Hartman, Michelle translator.
Title: The ninety-ninth floor / Jana Fawaz Elhassan ; translated by Michelle Hartman.
Other titles: Tābiq 99. English
Description: Northampton, MA : Interlink Books, 2016.
Identifiers: LCCN 2016034001 | ISBN 9781566560542 (pbk.)
Classification: LCC PJ7930.J36 T3313 2016 | DDC 892.7/37--dc23
LC record available at https://lccn.loc.gov/2016034001

Printed and bound in the United States of America

This book has been translated partially with the assistance of the Sharjah International Book Fair Translation Grand Fund.

To request our complete 48-page catalog, please call us
toll free at 1-800-238-LINK,
visit our website at www.interlinkbooks.com, or write to
Interlink Publishing, 46 Crosby Street, Northampton, MA 01060

Perhaps home is not a place but simply an irrevocable condition.

—James Baldwin

Part One

-I-

New York, Spring 2000

When I first got together with Hilda, I used to enjoy contemplating her reflection in the mirror for hours. I would intentionally take her to cafés and other places filled with mirrors. I'd look at her features in the mirror more than I'd gaze at her directly, as if purposely creating a distance between the physical being that was ostensibly her and her reflection, because a person's mirror image reveals more of who they really are; it reveals, in fact, the inner self, and to look upon that, as gratifying as it is, requires extraordinary courage.

Most of the time I would first steal a glance at her honey-colored eyes, and then move down to her delicate nose and full lips, and then finally settle on that little space between the two. Something between a woman's nose and upper lip always used to seduce me—perhaps it's the suppleness there. So did the length of the fingers and the size of the palm, as if a woman's hand could reveal what the rest of her body conceals.

I used to meditate on Hilda's face until she'd look at me, and I'd turn my gaze away from her, directing it once again at the mirror. When I retreated into myself I used to always compare the Hilda I could touch and her reflection—until I went mad and was having sex with her in front of the mirror, asking her to observe herself and really watch the movement of her body. I found her turning to look shyly at her bum and all the way to the bottom of her knees, and she would smile and bury her head in the nearest part of my body. In those moments her long, soft, brown hair would spread over her shoulders and my arms. She looked like a refugee who had turned her back on life and was sheltering in me.

For some reason I still can't figure out, when Hilda started getting off on the mirror game, I started hating it. I wished I'd never taught it to her. In the beginning it was as if she'd discovered my secret or had stolen my concept about people's truths and their reflections. I used to fear that she would be able to reach far beyond her naked self and realize her full potential, all of those things that most people remain ignorant of their entire lives.

Another thing changed when Hilda started looking in the mirror. I started being impotent. I couldn't enjoy the mirror reflection game and I burned with anger whenever she lifted her head to look at herself when we were having sex. I would wait for the minutes to pass, for her to feel shy and bury her head in my body as she always used to do. Those minutes grew longer time after time. Hilda no longer sheltered in my body after looking at us while we were making love. Instead, she started shooting me sharp looks and pulling me toward her. I would enter her violently until she would surrender and fade away in my arms.

My little girl started to run away from me after I had taught her to pursue herself. I had disclosed my secret to her without meaning to, like a fool or an idiot. The more I stared in mirrors, the more I gazed at her and focused on her, the more, in fact, I confronted myself. Now she'd open her eyes, which she used to keep closed when I was kissing her, and I no longer felt satisfied except when she'd surrender to darkness as if an indication of her total immersion in lovemaking and being completely cut off from the outside world.

A long time had passed since I'd looked at my own face. For a short time, I'd almost forgotten the scar that reached from my eye to the bottom of my left cheek. The truth is that I don't try to ignore this permanent defect in my physical condition. But I really did forget it was there sometimes, totally, just as we overlook many things in life. We don't call them back to memory except by chance or if time requires us to do so.

I forgot many things with Hilda, as if one day they just weren't there: The markets of Sabra and Shatila, the stench of sweat of the people walking by. The crowded houses, which looked like cardboard boxes all stuck together; and the random rooms the people of the camp added on to them later, when the land became too cramped and constricted. "Cramped, constricted land"—that's how my cousin Muhammad, who lived "over there," described it. Angry land, which seemed like it was preparing to swallow us up, disgruntled with us, not because we were occupying it but because both we and it shared our misery equally and we both hoped to escape. They threw us on that land and we threw ourselves on it. We and the cement were both detained within a few kilometers that could never embrace our past and our memories but that by default did become our present without being our future. This is what a refugee camp is—not a house or a home, but an overcrowded place, nothing more.

I forgot the scar on my face, my disabled leg, and the pain the doctor warned me I might not be able to bear. I forgot the weight of my body, daily concerns, and exhaustion. Did I forget, or was I pretending to forget? Forgetfulness is but a temporary disabling of pain; wheels will only turn again to reach the next station.

Between the two stops, the train was approaching its destination. My girlfriend and I were holding each other's hands, as if certain that our hearts had left each other's. We tried to capture each other's hearts in our hands, or use them to hold onto the sparks of the early days of love so they wouldn't disappear, and suddenly they took to flame and, then, burned out.

Time passed quickly when I was waiting to see her again. I smiled to myself and invented conversations of a sort we rarely had.

Even waiting for Hilda was not a burden, but a space occupied by the pleasure of imagining her: What clothes would she have on: one of her flowing skirts or her favorite purple sweater? What perfume? Would she interrogate me to see if I knew its scent and be enraged if I didn't? How would she move her mouth while eating? How many times would she laugh? What would she tell me about her friends? What would she complain about? Would she show me some innovative new dance move, and would she sit me on the sofa so I could enjoy watching her swaying body?

Whenever I thought about Hilda, I felt as though what remained of those cells of my skin that had sloughed off my face, leaving the scar, had given birth to fresh, new cells. I felt my skin emanating from beneath my flesh, my regenerated blood blooming all white and red so I became suddenly beautiful.

However, since my little girl decided to distance herself from me a bit, after repeatedly complaining about my continual absences she started looking for ways to fill her time. I started suffocating every time I hugged her, pulled her toward me, held her tightly; it felt as if something, an airless space, kept our bodies from fusing together. She would tense her belly backward, refusing to join together with me. I started feeling that even in the moments when we were closest and most intimate, that space, that gap between us wasn't just keeping us apart but was also pushing her away, far from me.

I used to wake up in the middle of the night and sit on the edge of my bed contemplating her, half of her body wrapped up and the other half exposed, wanting to wake her up and talk to her for a long time. I knew I could easily just make noise and she would sense my insomnia and ask me if everything was OK. This happened dozens of times. All I had to do was feign a cough or pretend that I was getting up to pour myself a glass of water, and she would open her eyes and reach out to me to check on me and see if I was there. I would ask her any silly question to start a conversation, a conversation that would sometimes last until dawn.

After Hilda listened to my chatting, I would always be able to once again surrender to a deep sleep—eyes closed, anxiety-free, immersed in incomparable comfort. I didn't really notice that, after those late night talks, my love was unable to go back to sleep. When she was lying next to me, it never occurred to me to think about what she was dreaming or even to ask myself if I had stolen her sleep, cut off the dreams she'd been sailing in. I simply used to just feel satiated—that I had unloaded a huge burden and could once again go forward.

No longer did I dare to violate her sleep. My hands would automatically start to tremble if I so much as tried to touch her hair or stroke it gently. She would fall asleep here, in my bed, one inch from my arm, which seemed so far away. As if I wouldn't ever reach her again, as if an entire era would pass by, my lips begging her for a kiss or a word to calm me down. Even if she kept calling me "habibi" until the end of time, I would never feel as I did before. Her being here, acting like this, was a punishment that I wasn't sure I deserved.

I got out of bed and went to the door, which I'd leaned my crutch against, but I didn't pick it up. I left it there and started moving around the house on my weak leg, deliberately walking faster and planting my feet on the ground, as if I hoped that the lower part of my body, specifically the left side, would stumble on the marble to relieve itself of its heavy load.

For a moment, certain that what I was doing wouldn't lead to the desired result, I thought that perhaps I was trying to prove to myself again that I am that man of steel whom nothing can stop from walking, carrying on, moving forward. I was now challenging my body, as I was apt to do sometimes—fighting with it, cursing it, getting angry at it. And yet at other times I was kind to it, embracing it.

Afterward, I got tired and hurt my leg until it became so numb that I lost all feeling in it. I stretched out on the big red sofa that Hilda had chosen for the sitting room, along with honey-colored chairs and a wood table in the middle. Actually, Hilda had chosen all the furniture for the house when she moved in with me. Crystal vases, silver bowls and plates, cherry- and mulberry-scented candles for the décor, and new, colorful curtains, as well as orange and white ceramics for the washroom. She turned everything upside down.

Even though I had become relatively well off after suffering years of deprivation, I'd never enjoyed sophisticated taste: it's something comfortable people are born with and poor people can't ever acquire. Most of the time I bought regular white sheets and inappropriate furniture. I never realized how dull the house's ambiance was until she changed it. Gloomy olive green and dark brown wood, which overshadowed most parts of the house, were like an extension of my old house—as if I had transported the camp here without meaning to.

I smiled when I looked at the place, and the pain in my foot subsided. It was a victor's smile. I started to hum an Andalusian tune to keep my loneliness company and relieve some of the weight of my memories.

Singing is also resistance. Don't people in prisons and jails do it instead of complaining? For them, it can be an occasional sliver of light, a way to trick their bodies into producing sound, reminding them that their voices are still there… As I kept humming I thought about all the detainees denied their freedom. Sleep finally took hold, and with it came a dream, a dream that my singing was directed at them, joined up with theirs. Our voices rose up, in unison, to break down their cell doors.

-2-

Hilda woke me up in the morning, massaging my face with her fingers, whispering my name to rouse me from my slumber. "Majd … Majd … Majdi," she kept repeating my name until I opened my eyes and looked at her. She smiled. I smiled back, and silence settled upon us for a few seconds.

"I made you coffee. Look, I got you a new mug." She pointed at where she'd put it. It was a big white mug, with the words "Big Hug Mug" written on it in English in large red letters. "It's a Kate Spade design, I bought it yesterday from a shop in Times Square. Actually I bought a lot of things: earrings for my mother and sister from Tiffany's. You know how my mother is—her gift has to be from the fanciest jewelry shop so she can brag about it to her lady friends.… Why aren't you saying anything? Don't you like the mug?" She was talking quickly, as if trying to avoid the main subject. She knew it and so did I. But we were putting off talking, and putting off acknowledging what we knew. She told me calmly the previous week that she intended to go back to Beirut for a visit that might be extended, depending on how things went.

"What things?" I asked her. "What things? You have nothing to do there. Your life is here. Your work is here. Your home is here. Why are you going there?"

Hilda didn't answer, as if giving me a greater chance to object to her trip. "And me? Haven't you thought about the impact of your absence on me if you're away for a long time?" My girlfriend indulged in a long silence as if to draw me into even more moaning and begging her to stay, and at that moment I ascertained that I was responding the way she wanted me to. I pursed my lips, turned my glance away from her, and stopped talking.

A few minutes of total silence passed before Hilda took the initiative to justify her trip, talking about her continual struggle between "over here" and "over there." She told me that she desperately needed to go back, that in order to understand where she is now she needed to face up to that place. She said that she felt alienated and out of place, that the weight of the time she'd spent far away from her memories felt harsh and agonizing. She then started assuring me that she would come back and that her going wasn't an attempt to escape from our love.

"I'm not leaving you. I simply need to go to my country, even if only for a few weeks. I need you to understand me right now. Nothing will undermine our love."

"Our love won't be able to carry on when you go, it'll die.... You'll be immersed in their world and you'll believe what they'll tell you about me."

"That won't happen."

"What will you say? I'm in love with a crippled Palestinian guy?"

"I won't say anything. I'm not going there to say something. Try to understand. You aren't just a 'crippled Palestinian guy.' You're the man I love."

"Go. But your going away will mean many things."

"Are you threatening me?"

"I'm just informing you, that's all."

She tried to look at me defiantly, but brokenness and sadness filled her eyes. She looked as if she were trying to resist arguing with me, to supplicate in silence. Perhaps at a given moment she wanted me to reassure her—to tell her that there's plenty of room in her memory for us to fill together and that I was desperate to stand up for "us" as a couple—to beg her to stay in New York, to persuade her that she belongs to this country, and that Uncle Sam won't ever want her to leave. But I didn't do it, and with deliberate cruelty, I told her that I wished her good luck, that I would try to wait for her. I filled the emptiness with my own kind of confrontation. When I told her this full of arrogance and swagger, not at all how a lover should tell his beloved that he would be there when she finished her journey of facing up to her past. Or that he would still be close to her while she was away.

I looked at her viciously. I fixed my gaze on her shoulders, and then lifted my eyes until my face was equal to hers. We kept staring at each other, each peering into the other's eyes as if we were waiting to see who would turn their gaze away from the other first, exactly like a duel. I wanted her to close her eyes, to grieve and be afraid. But I saw her just like that, refusing to retreat. That's what excited me.

At that moment we seemed adrift, and in dire need

of an embrace to help our bodies forcefully fuse together. Desire orbited around us, at some times fierce and at others weak and submissive. I was staring at Hilda's shoulders, how they were in perfect harmony with her neck, and wishing I could pull her to my chest and tell her how beautiful she was, how much I desired to keep her here with me, right next to my heart. But I didn't do that. I told her instead that I would comply with her decision, so as to act like a civilized man who had yielded to the notion of loss by pretending to accept it magnanimously.

In the following days, while she was packing her things and preparing for her trip, I observed her from afar as she folded her dresses carefully and arranged them in her suitcase. I was terrified, afraid of the idea that the house would be emptied of her things, that I wouldn't see the drops of water on her toothbrush in the morning and wouldn't find her hairs stuck in the comb on the table or her underwear lying on the floor.

In that period, the idea of her taking up space in my clothes closet with her things no longer bothered me, indeed I considered telling her that she could take everything, that she could shove me over to the edge of the bed and pull all the covers over to her side and watch all the programs that she liked on television and that I wouldn't object to any of this, as long as she would still be there and I would be able to rest my head against her in the evening, when she fell asleep and the world went quiet.

I remembered the previous evening, how she pulled my head to her chest and lay it near her heart. She didn't say anything but she cried. Her tears weren't heavy, but they were focused. One drop after another fell at intervals.

Each one fell on my head like a whole tribe of tears, as if it were itself a story—a great love story that accused me of not understanding and that I killed with my own hands.

Just then I felt like a cat eating its young out of fear for them, especially if they were born with delicate constitutions. But she stayed here in that moment and I did, too; I didn't swallow her up. Why did hope in restoring our love abate? Why did she have to go if her farewell would be so tearful?

"I'm not crying because of you, I'm crying because of myself.... I'm sure you'll understand one day."

But I didn't understand a thing, especially women's insistence on ambiguity. I didn't know what could have been so enticing about a past she'd decided she didn't belong to. I didn't understand either nostalgia or the impossibility of seceding from memory. I used to think she was different, like those hard-to-find women who kick away everything that might violently pull them toward bad memories and don't look back. One day, I saw her aim such a kick at me, and I thought that preemptively abandoning her might help me avoid the torture that was surely coming.

When her departure date came, I stood in our building's entryway, watching the driver put her suitcases into the car. I started thinking about tricks I could pull that might block her exit, like locking the building's entrances and exits and pretending to lose the keys, or even puncturing the tires to prevent her from getting to the airport on time, but in my heart I was incapable of taking a tough stance on her decision because I wanted her to remain close to me voluntarily.

My impression that she needed me, desired me—that

her eyes shone from just thinking about me—was the only thing guaranteed to motivate me to work miracles for her to be happy and therefore to stay with me. The only thing that would crush me more than her abandoning me was the possibility she would stay here out of pity.

It was possible that this would constitute the knockout punch that would completely paralyze me: my impression that Hilda was deluding me and herself, that she felt forced to take care of me out of humanitarianism or to avoid feeling guilty over leaving an antisocial, physically handicapped man with a limp and a scar on his face. That would confirm that I was indeed deficient—that I needed a medical caretaker, not a woman. I didn't want to classify myself as handicapped or incapacitated. That's what I'd fought against for so much of my life.

I wanted her to see me as her man who was complete, to feel that she was a woman with me—a woman from the top of her head to the tips of her toes—not a project for a nurse who's a companion to a prematurely gray old man. I wanted her to tremble when she touched me, like a little bird in its nest shaded by its mother's wings, or a little kitten whose owner took her by surprise and startled her by petting her fur.

That could perhaps make a difference in my behavior toward her, to become more refined and act correctly. I used to wish that on her trip, she would awaken to the fact that she had become my prey and had grown to love her cage so much over time that it would become her home, that she would be sure that escaping would destroy her, and so she would come back and overwhelm me with kisses. Then she would laugh like she always used to do when she discovered that I was right but didn't want to admit it.

-3-

New York, JFK, 2000

Hilda left. She was wearing a transparent white shirt and skinny jeans. She dragged two large purple suitcases behind her. She left, and I kept staring at the airport lobby, as if I couldn't believe she'd gone and was hoping she'd come back. I watched her pulling the suitcases and looking back, waving at me until she was lost in the crowd of travelers.

I looked around myself imagining she would appear from behind a door, and my eye fell upon the John F. Kennedy Airport sign. I was lost in thought about this inimitable character and I don't know why I started comparing him to myself. I remembered his heroism as the captain of the American PT boat 109 when it crashed into an iron war ship in 1943 and how he brought nine members of his crew to safety after long nights behind Japanese lines. This incident not only transformed him into a national hero but also compromised his physical health and later disabled him. There are two sides to every tragedy—one heroic, another devastating, as if greatness must be equated with misery and pain.

I kept waiting, like this, for thirty minutes, without looking at my watch even once. My wait was part of an attempt to absorb what was happening, as if my mind had stopped working, as if I were dissociated from my body and was only able to sit on an airport chair, resigned to its desire for complete apathy. Only when someone's carry-on bag fell down near me, making an irritating noise did I notice how long I'd stayed there. Only then did I raise my eyes from the floor. It seemed like everyone was getting ready to travel or waiting to meet their loved ones like a gang or a bunch of accomplices. Why hadn't they stopped her from going? An unprecedented hatred for everything and everyone around me came over me and I wanted to scream at all those strangers that a hole had been bored in my chest the moment the plane took off, a hole I know would expand with every mile the plane flew. These feelings of loss afflict people and handicap them like threadbare clothing, leaving them totally empty, incomplete, and angry. So I was a shirt that could perhaps be mended but would never again to return to how it was originally.

Hilda was now gone. I'd resolved to get control over my anger and not blame her for my suffering, to respect her need to get away for a while, as I promised her I would. Implicitly I only wanted to smash the ideal of the civilized man who accepts loss magnanimously and considers it a part of life to console himself. I wanted to pull her by the hair and drag her back to me, to plant her between my legs and make her stay here, to shut her up if she tried to complain, to make love with her like a whole, complete man, then wrap her up in my arms so she could sleep satisfied and content.

I want to say that I am not that perfect man and that a destructive beast is also hidden within me, finding refuge there, and that from time to time I feel an urgent desire to expel it, when it swells under my skin and my pain becomes much too strong to fight against. But what could I do to take revenge on Hilda? Nothing. I could only cut myself off from her, and not answer the phone when she called to check on me. That was my only way to punish her, if I dared to do it.

The whole way back home from the airport, I was thinking about the meaning of both loss and our thinking that we are entitled to people—that at a given moment we feel that those close to us are not allowed to leave our daily lives. I tried to trick myself into some kind of idealism by thinking that absence also has another side, that it enhances the presence of love and confirms its usefulness, and also by thinking that space between lovers is necessary, that life will take its natural course with time, and that after a while destiny will bring those who we need close to our hearts.

Surely I imagined loss to be something temporary, a phase that occurred at particular moments in life. Since my ideas fluctuated between the positive and negative, I started thinking that loss perhaps was also eternal. Why else would the shadow of death always haunt us and take away the ones we love? Why do some images of our loved ones after they die remain frozen in our in our minds in a fixed, static, temporal frame? Was it possible that the picture imprinted in my memory of Hilda leaving in a crowd of travelers was the last one?

There surely had to be another end to the story even

if it meant I had to follow her, join her where she was, talk to her, and explain everything that I never did when she was in New York. Perhaps if I went "over there," to that place I was determined to forget, I would find other words or even a new outlet for words or a language that perhaps would seem more compelling and attractive. This is what I'd sought my whole life, to create pictures, to reject them when they came like this, to insist on life whenever I could and to reduce the impact of pain.

It wasn't possible to submit to such a ridiculous ending, like Hilda phoning me from Beirut having realized that she didn't love me and that her roots had suddenly grown deeper into the earth with her nostalgic return to her motherland. Wasn't this what people always said—either that all those trips and stations along the way are more than merely travel, or that at some point returning becomes inevitable?

I was only trying to resist returning and to erase the past from my memory as if it never happened. I was trying to forget my identity and the country I didn't know, to deny my affiliation to any fixed geographical spot.

I was also here, in the greatest country in the world. Every day I passed by the Empire State Building. I stared at its 102 floors in awe and wished that buildings would succeed in finding their way to the sky, so that if I stood on the highest floor of a building or a tower, I also would belong to "the top." Every other place would be lower—Beirut and the Palestine I'd never known.

From here, when I looked at the world from the balcony of my office on the ninety-ninth floor of the building, the camp wasn't there anymore. Palestine was like a country lost in the crowd, a country whose entreaties couldn't reach me, if it dared to try to make them. My office was the place in which I exercised my power—intimate and domesticated, arrogant and overbearing, all at the same time. Even if I had failed in choosing my household furniture, my workplace décor was something altogether different.

A sleek, oval-shaped, modern office, black and white marble floors. Sitting near the door, a bust of Venus, the Roman goddess of love, beauty, and fertility. A gray sofa extended all along the wall, matched by a glass table that reflected the room's light, the newest Apple laptop sitting atop it, along with booklets explaining the video games that the company created.

For me, my office was the ultimate unrivaled place, linked to adventure, departure, discovery, and the impunity of power and innovation. But it also could be a hell—whenever I threw ideas and effort into it, it wanted more. A savage place opening its smiling mouth to suck you into the flow of speed and production, to invent tricks and characters for you in turn to suck children into this terrible, fast-paced world.

It was a world trying to avert your gaze but at the same time holding your fascination in its grips and so you would continue to indulge in it to the end. "Formula One," a driving game we'd recently designed, for example, gave those children—and grownups too—a feeling of power. They could be professional drivers: driving their cars off course and then returning them to the right path, even if they crashed into other cars and suffered horrible accidents. The game made them feel that their sins were forgiven and that destruction wouldn't stop them from reaching the finish line. Speed alone was important, the ability to overcome adversity at the highest possible velocity.

Up high in that building I felt like I was eternally running away toward greatness. For a long time I succeeded in forgetting, or pretending to forget, so many things before Hilda came along and changed everything. It was as if she, with a lot of love, cracked my hard shell and left me naked in a room full of mirrors. I returned home. I looked at my face in the mirror. And I saw nothing but shrapnel.

-4-

Lebanon, 1982, Sabra and Shatila Camp

"Yamma! Mama!"

"What's up?"

"Daddy keeps saying we have to go to Auntie Zahra's house in Burj Camp.... He wants to tell you that it's going to be a hard night."

"Why won't he come and stay with us? How will we get to your Auntie Zahra's house?"

My mother wasn't even able to finish her questions before we could feel the shelling and bombardment that had begun to hit our area from all sides. She was heavily pregnant and she couldn't move easily. Part of her flowing, striped dress was dragging behind her.

She moved around the kitchen, washed the dishes, and dried them with a cheap towel frayed from the many times she had boiled it in the big aluminum pot she used to bleach clothes and towels.

She heard the sound of gunfire erupting outside, shut the doors to the house tightly and put her hand on her belly. She mumbled words I didn't understand, cursed war and the diaspora, and then went back to the kitchen to take out some potatoes and start peeling them. I couldn't understand her amazing ability to carry on with all the sounds reverberating outside, as if she were used to the idea of warfare, deliberately creating a space outside of it to allow her to keep on living.

My heartbeat quickened and I went in to pull her by the dress to leave the potatoes, stop moving, and recognize that things weren't going well. She turned toward me and said that we would wait until the situation calmed down a bit, and then we'd go to my Auntie Zahra's house. We heard loud knocking at the door, accompanied by my father's shouting, telling us to open up quickly. She left the potatoes and the peels in the sink. Bits of dirt were still stuck to her hands. She wiped them on her dress, took out the keys, and asked my father to calm down.

"May God destroy them!"

"Now's not the time for prayers. As soon as the situation calms down we'll go to Burj camp. I left the guys and came straight to you."

"Now you come? You've been away five days!"

"Listen, woman, this isn't the time for reproaches!"

My father's anxious tone kept ringing in my ears, like I imagined it was when he was carrying me in his arms when I was injured in the leg by the bomb blast. I was wounded because I went out to bring some things my father had left in front of the house when he came unexpectedly—a suitcase and two bags. I didn't know what was in them; I don't know how it happened so fast. I saw blood pouring off me, including my face. I didn't know just then that shrapnel had hit me there as well. My father ran toward me. My mother screamed and started telling him to take me to the Gaza Hospital. I was in his arms and he rushed to get me medical help, my blood mixing with the sweat pouring off of his forehead before I totally lost consciousness.

"The boy's going to die in our arms.... Go! I'll take care of myself."

"How can I just go, how will you get out?"

"Go, I'm telling you, just go."

My father left. He carried me far from death but he wasn't able to get back to my mother and the baby who hadn't yet seen the light of day. Flare bombs surrounded the Shatila refugee camp afterward and the genocide started. Corpses were piled up on the ground and my father couldn't go back, he couldn't penetrate the human rubble and save my mother.

If only she'd left with us. If only she'd gotten to my Auntie Zahra's house first. If only she hadn't been pregnant. Perhaps then my father's face wouldn't have changed after the massacre and he wouldn't have transformed from that militant hero into a broken man whom the war and its tragedies had annihilated.

Going backward: September 16, 1982, at precisely five PM, the massacre began. It's impossible to memorize this date as merely a number. Indeed its images are almost constantly dying and being reborn. In an attempt to restore memory, events always seem scattered and incomplete, for no reason but their sheer horror.

In my head, the massacre is always linked to silence, except that my father escaped with me before the bombardment stopped and the camp's soul was severed. The severity of a massacre isn't only about the destruction but also the idea of returning there, to a place reeking of the dead, a place stifling their voices, depriving them even of their death rattles, rejecting their having been killed.

The peeled potatoes, the pots women had put on the stove, the laundry hanging on clotheslines, the trash bags waiting for someone to take them out—all things that froze one day on that land, as did everything people didn't come back for.

This tragedy, like all tragedies of war, didn't end after these events. Instead it started there, with tales of buried body parts and corpses that hadn't bid farewell to life on their sick beds with a smile, as we're used to seeing in films, but rather with panicked stares, with begging and pleading.

The massacre I saw later in pictures and the accounts of some of the survivors made death for me transform into an image of a butcher, a knife, and eyes filled with fear. Even if I heard about someone passing away naturally, from an illness, for example, I could only imagine a dead person like that—with knife or gunshot wounds. This image itself was enough to enrage me and make me forever hope to die asleep in bed with my eyes closed.

My father carried me, searching for a way out, before the camp was completely besieged. That morning a strange smell engulfed the camp. We were mice who sensed there was a trap somewhere, a trap whose existence there was no evidence of. I escaped before the camp was under siege and the killing started.

I don't know how my mother was killed that day. Or if one of the gunmen raped her. Or if they split open her belly because she was pregnant, as they did to many other women. I don't know what happened to the potatoes.

What the neighbors reported—those who were left to tell what happened—was that our neighbor Fawzi's sister was crawling toward her murdered mother's breast to take it in her mouth when soldiers opened fire on her too. Our neighbor Said tried to resist them and they kicked him in the testicles and spat on him to death. At the time I couldn't grasp the meaning of the expression "spat on him to death." Spitting doesn't kill. But insults do. No one knew anything about my mother. They didn't leave us any narration of her murder. No one said if her screaming rang out throughout the place. No one counted the bullets that hit her. No one said a thing.

Our neighbor Abu Hassan miraculously survived because he was able to hide in the attic closet. He was alone at home when heard gunmen outside. He couldn't search for his children and his wife. He knew that the moment he left the house would be his last. "The hardest thing in the world is to know that the people you love are being murdered next to you and you can't do a thing about it," he told my father, painfully biting his lower lip and curling his lips to expose a lone golden tooth shining among his other, Arabic-tobacco, cigarette-stained teeth.

The gunmen had entered his home and turned it upside down, he recalled, while he was holding his breath above them. He felt handicapped, on the ground for hours with water a couple of meters from him and him unable to reach it—either by crawling or walking. "We aren't men," he told my father, "we aren't anything at all."

There are many stories of death after the massacre. Women slap the sides of their faces and curse the Arabs and Arab nationalism. Dead bodies packed into plastic bags and nameless corpses buried under the dirt. Black bags containing intact corpses if the dead person was lucky. If not, body parts. Sometimes perhaps, so-and-so's hand is put with so-and-so else's foot. No difference. The important thing was to finish completing the death scene. Mass graves were dug to put dead bodies in, without the right to a decent funeral.

"Where is my mother?" I asked my father after I knew what had happened. He didn't answer. "Where's her body?" Silence. "Dad, what happened to the baby?" Silence. He didn't say a thing. Days passed; he didn't answer.

A little while afterward, when his wound had healed a bit, I started asking him about her, and he would say, "Your mother went to Palestine to give birth there.... Your mother went to Palestine and we are all going to go back to Palestine." This is how he would respond to my annoying questioning without being specific about the date of return—this return that he kept dreaming about—like someone who actually believed his own deception was real, the lie told to a child who wasn't yet fifteen years old.

My father kept himself alive by hoping to return to the Galilee, convinced that my mother didn't die, that she was waiting for us in Kfar Yasif and that she would introduce us to the baby, eager to see us. He would carry on describing my brother, as if he were sure that the baby my mother was carrying inside her was a boy, which I somehow couldn't be sure of. Listening to my father was invariably confusing—were his words true or false? It was of course a shame for me to confront him with my doubts, but once I hinted to him that I knew the truth and that

I was completely fine with our reality. I whispered to him that I knew why he was suddenly so sad.

"No, I'm not sad. What do you know? Tell me!"

"I know but I won't say."

"Yes you will, you have to tell me what you know."

"But I don't want to talk."

He insisted I tell him what I meant by claiming this knowledge, what I was hiding from him. But at the time I felt as if I were responsible for him, as if we had traded roles as father and son for a few moments. He was the son whose feelings it was hard to hurt by informing him that I was fully aware of the death of my mother and the baby.

It's as if I were the one who had to lighten the burden of his loss, so I told him that I knew that my mother had gone ahead of us to Kafr Yasif, because I'd heard the neighbors saying it. I gave him a new pretext for denial, and he hugged me and patted my head, saying, "She's waiting there. Didn't I tell you she was waiting there?" We then both sunk into a long silence. I thought he would continue like this for ages.

Later, my father broke the silence and started talking about the Nakba and the losses of 1948, when he was still a teenager, almost fifteen years old, the same age I was on the day of the massacre. My father also used to tell me a story going back before the Nakba, in 1939, when, during the Mandate, the British burned down many houses in the village because of the murder of two of their soldiers. He was only six years old, but the image of the two fires was seared into his memory. Afterward, he knew that one of the burned houses had belonged to Adonis Nasra, a close friend of his father, my grandfather.

"Kafr Yasif was the capital of the Galilee. We didn't believe the English would go and let the Jews come. The English terrorized us, and then they burned Adonis Nasra's house and the letters he'd sent to his brother in Mexico. Adonis couldn't find his brother anymore. He was lost and I guess is still lost."

My father pretended that escaping Kafr Yasif had never happened, omitting the details of the trip to recall only that he'd found himself in Lebanon. His denial of the geographical distance he had crossed to arrive at the border was a denial of his displacement and a desire to believe that he'd arrived in South Lebanon by accident, like a man who'd wandered off and lost his home address but would surely go back one day.

-5-

New York, Spring 2000

My mother is in the Galilee. I also like to believe that she is there, so I don't fall apart by dramatizing the tragedy of her loss. My father is in a cemetery far from his land. Hilda went "over there." I am in New York, standing on the balcony of my office on the ninety-ninth floor. I see my reflection in the glass, far above the city of light, and I think that surely these foreigners must feel we are strangers.

There is no Arab land on which to stand, no cause or struggle. A city turns its wheels quickly, and leaves you alone in a vast ocean, always needing a lot of kindling to ignite its fuel. Perhaps the analogy isn't accurate. Kindling has a scent, land, and soil, and soil itself needs a homeland. I am here in the vast ocean they call "New York," which always needs its buttons pressed to keep its wheels turning. I walk through the streets of this big city and just when I feel that I know them, I find some corner that makes me realize I've lost my way, that the only road here is nowhere, and that I need to erase my Arab facial features in order to be someone, in order to become someone.

This Kafr Yasif that I never knew, that I had googled many times to see some pictures of and succeeded only in finding a few snapshots of, never revealed any trace of my mother. What is she doing where she is now? Is she wearing her navy blue and white striped dress, with its fine gray embroidery? Is she peeling potatoes? Why do I still not have even one picture of her? I type the words "Kafr Yasif" into an Internet search and it informs me that it's a "town in the Galilee district in Israel." Another site says that the city is celebrated in zajal poetry, which sings of its ancient buildings. I look at the images: buildings and houses, some of which have red-tiled roofs. Cars. Faces. People. No trace of my mother.

I confess that I never felt a sweeping nostalgia for my homeland until after I met Hilda. I found myself telling her the details of my imagination about that place. Details I myself didn't realize were there in my mind. With my love, I would talk a lot about places, memories, tragedies, massacres, businessmen, and business deals. Every time I told her about an incident or a thought, I felt as if I were getting to know myself for the first time—like a man who is coming alive, emerging from the depths and making everything that had been sunk into oblivion float up to the surface. As if when we talk about ourselves, we realize how much we are strangers to ourselves.

I told her about my return to the camp after the massacre and after I had recovered a bit, about our little house that was left in ruins. There was blood everywhere, the sofa was turned upside down.... There was a pot on the stove. Potatoes and potato peels on the floor. She had definitely sprinkled them with salt to fry them and put them to one side. My mother had also prepared soup that day, before she knew that none of us would eat it. For the longest time, I used ask myself if the gunmen had tasted it or dipped their fingers in it.

My Auntie Zahra came with us to clean the house and pack up my mother's things, but my father asked her to leave the cupboard as it was. When I saw her organizing the place, I thought that women have an amazing ability to face up to death, superior to that of men. I felt that my father was fragile glass as she put on yellow plastic gloves, washed the dishes, and cleaned the windows. And then moved to the floor. She threw water on it and started scrubbing the tiles, scratching off the remaining stains with her bare fingernails.

I didn't know I could recall this much detail until I told Hilda what happened to us. I recalled corners and colors I thought irrevocably buried. But I could see even my auntie's black dress and her white scarf, as if I were still there. Whenever I would imagine her, I would see her in the same dress, as if she never, ever took it off.

Not only was the past exhumed in front of Hilda but also the present and my relationship to America. She brought me new information and introduced me to a whole new world: her strange people, people who were often likely to be enemies to my reality. But I wanted her to talk about them so I could try to know them through her. Perhaps in fact I wanted this to reassure myself at certain moments that she wasn't one of them, that at the end of the day she would leave them, taking revenge on them for me. Then Hilda would become all mine.

When she would scream, "Please, for the Virgin Mary's sake!" as she always did when she was surprised, I'd then wait for her to let out her extended, ringing laugh, while hiding her lips behind her fingers and intensifying the sparkle in her eyes, which expressed her happiness.

She wasn't the kind of woman who would laugh only with her mouth, but instead one of those women whose heart jumps in place as if it's rejoicing. When she couldn't stop laughing, her whole body and even feet would shake and she would put her hand on my shoulder. This would always end with her embracing me and smiling when her cheek touched my face. I would sniff at her, as if wanting to breathe in this woman so as to keep her in that embrace indefinitely.

Talking to Hilda used to give me boundless comfort. She made me feel that I could dwell on my words and thoughts without being observed. I used to negate even my usual self to feel that I was superior to her. When I used to tell her tales of my friends and relatives—or even private things about myself—I always used to discover secrets.

I told Hilda about my Lebanese friend Mohsen who came to live in this country during the Civil War. When I described his long hair and his beard, which he grew so as to be distinctive and physically striking, I paid attention for the first time to the fact that Mohsen—who'd become Mike in the land of skyscrapers—and his beard seemed to impress his American friends. In a different context, this beard itself would perhaps have been scary and made them feel threatened. But Mike's beard was a fashion statement that impressed some of them so much that they imitated it.

"Arabs' beards are different because they can conceal weapons...." I told Hilda. "A beard can be a cache for death; the space between the little hairs can hide a trap or grenade. You know, even shaykhs, bishops, and monks' beards are different than Mike's beard." After telling her this, I felt I wanted to discover the world with her. She and I started analyzing the meaning of beards, how throughout the ages they had been grown as a sign of wisdom, elevated rank, or sexual prowess.

"I think Mike wanted to give the appearance of strength, not just to be different," she told me and was silent for a second before I agreed with her. So in this way Mohsen really was tirelessly gathering strength. He wanted that flashiness—not power or authority. That's what always fascinated him about New York.

Though this country enjoys the most authority in the world, it is power that attracted him to it. "What's the difference between the two? Aren't they complementary? Or at least related?" Hilda asked me. I answered, "There's a big difference. Power is built from inside and leads you to authority, which is a mix of life experience, containing a lot of losses not just gains. Authority! Authority is the disaster, in particular that authority which engenders power. Then it results in blindly destructive power that acknowledges no deterrents."

Despite its authority that extends all the way up to the end of the sky, New York is an exemplar of a certain power, undeniable, solid, hard as steel. To me, the deep texture of this power stems from its unity and synergy. And a fast-paced life—there's no room to waste time here.

It feeds on the desire to stay and meet all those needs that force people to not look at the sun, which is eclipsed in any case by high-rise buildings. It is a city of strangers: a place you don't belong to but can find yourself in. Most people who live here came from far away, and although each one of them has a different accent and a different story, they seem familiar with the place, as if at home.

I always ask myself if this guy Mike, who is so estranged from his Arabness and seeks refuge in the city lights, really belongs to this country. Perhaps in his moments of brilliance, the system transformed him into a New Yorker. He repeatedly tried to convince himself that "Mohsen" had died. To him, he doesn't exist anymore; he even changed the thin build of his body by working out and strengthening his muscles, whitened his teeth, and let his hair grow long. At a certain moment, he was forced to go back to being his old self, when the same system kicked him to the curb after which he woke up to find himself broke and at rock bottom. Mohsen, the Muslim, who lived through the Civil War with a sectarian identity like all Lebanese did, came back. The Lebanese weren't individuals or citizens, but only "Muslims and Christians." For me, his resistance, which let him hang on through his darkest hours, surely must have been Arab and a result of that war that itself generated inside people this ability to endure and survive.

He had some of that enduring patience, which we as people on the other side of the world have gotten used to. Mohsen was the one who remained strong, not Mike. Mohsen, who grew up in Beirut's alleys, between rifles and the sounds of cannons, was not this rich guy whose money multiplied only for it to escape him later, and leave him without the money-making machine that limits the economy to bank transactions and deals.

Mike never came back here either. He promised me he'd return after his crisis had passed. But now he was urging me to visit him, saying he couldn't come until all of his financial problems were over. Our American friend Marianne told me after she visited him in Lebanon that he was still as she had left him: crazy and passionate about life. He was still narcissistic and dreaming of bright city lights. He opened a little restaurant on a corner of Bliss Street in Beirut, planning for this simple place to become an international chain one day, sweeping away other fast food restaurants.

There, on that street, he kept his beard. He did things any regular worker would do: clean the floor, wash vegetables, cut meat, and bake bread in the oven. He used to do all this as entertainment, as if he'd found a new passion as a cook, and he'd ask those of his friends who'd tasted his recipes to sing his praises and solicited them to say that he had culinary skill and that his food was the most delicious they'd ever tried.

Here in New York, I would visualize the people around him who always looked alike. I could only imagine Mike's friends as one type, as marginal, cardboard people who came together and ate their food with silver spoons and forks using the same kinds of gestures. In my imagination, they would lift the food up to their mouths with a smile always drawn on cardboard mouths and swallow after chewing exactly three times. Sometimes they would talk in an unintelligible language, as if what they were saying was particular to cardboard or plastic puppets, with no significance or meaning.

Mike was a contradictory person who tried to keep himself surrounded by a lot of people. Women and men, male and female friends, appeared in his life day after day. Many of them disappeared, in the same way that they appeared, with the speed of lightning. The only ones who stayed close to him are those who were happy to put up with his volatile moods and temper, because they knew that deep down he was a good person who couldn't hurt anyone. I was really very different than his acquaintances, whether because of something particular and special about me, or because of my disability, I don't know. But I felt like I was the only one among them who could feel pain.

My physical form, tainted by many flaws, made me unusual; indeed, their constant staring at me betrayed what was going on in their minds: *What is this handicapped guy doing with Mike, who's always so chic and well-dressed?* After looking at me for a while, they stopped and went back to their conversations, as if thinking, *What do we have to do with that crippled guy's tragedy?*

Deep down, I never cared how they saw me. Indeed, their sense of superiority sometimes made my own sense of superiority toward them stronger, as if I were telling them, "What do you know about life, you silly people? Did it ever rough you up like it did me? What do you know about Mike? Do you even know that he's Mohsen?" That pain made me feel special but it could make me feel inferior at the same time.

Sometimes, when we were all together deep in a conversation and I felt one of them pat me on the shoulder,

I would forget my disability and figure they too had forgotten it. I'd smile and laugh, and those moments would help me recognize my distance from people, my sense of internalized alienation from them. I used to wonder if people were all really opinionated or if I was the one who was afraid, completely immersed in tragedy because I found some kind of belonging within it.

Perhaps my visit to Mike, and my persistence in connecting to his crazy, strange world, was a way to escape tragedy, to interact and create a normal life where there weren't all of these gaps between people, a life I wasn't embarrassed about, a life in which I felt neither superior nor inferior but, simply, balanced.

I felt attached to my Lebanese friend in part because I was perpetually dazzled by his ability to be unsettled and how he enjoyed this state of continual change. I used to always think about his strange ability to walk away from things. Sometimes I considered him a wise and serious person, only for his flightiness to return and flood his face. At some moments he seemed to be merely a selfish man, as if the goal of those people he kept around him was just to strengthen his narcissism, his desire to be a brilliant man and the center of attention.

To maintain your friendship with Mike you had to avoid trying to outdo him, never show yourself to be better than him, and always sing his praises. For this reason, my relationship with him was limited to weekly get-togethers, not daily contact that would necessitate sharing our private business.

I liked to visit him from time to time. I would listen to his tales of what was happening around him. Truthfully,

I didn't do that only out of love for him. I was curious about him. I also used to explore—even if only for a few minutes—that flightiness as a way of life; I, who am so encumbered by fears and worries; I, the man for whom it's hard to shake off the burden of taking himself so seriously.

Every time I paid him a visit, Mike would introduce me to a new woman: a lover, friend, girlfriend, even sometimes a wife. All of them had one thing in common: they were all blindly smitten by him and by his curiosity about them. Only one woman got the better of him and his propensity for excessive self-love—Eva, who was Mexican and herself dreamed of fame. This young woman resembled him somehow, except for one simple difference. He was fanciful and she was pragmatic. She set her boundaries and declared them viciously and unyieldingly.

When trying to figure out Mike's personality or the uniqueness of Mohsen's, it's worth mentioning my hesitancy to introduce him to Hilda at the beginning. He was that friend you couldn't trust but at the same time couldn't give up. I steered clear of introducing my girlfriend to him, especially when I first met her, back when I saw her as a young girl, a kitten who simply needed protection. She was alone here, coming from far away to study dance and fashion design. To me she was like a rose about to bloom, with a seductiveness she didn't know she had. She was one of those easily manipulated young women: a transparent crystal ball shining like a body that reflects that whole world in it.

She was from "over there," a place that carried the fragrance of childhood innocence. Timid beauty that always remains subtle but is delicately supplicating. At times it implores you to come near it and penetrate it, forces you to close your eyes, to stand trembling, afraid of spoiling it, exactly like schoolchildren try to keep their notebooks organized and clean at the beginning of the school year. Or how children write their first letters in their copybooks slowly and carefully and try to shape their handwriting symmetrically—they are keen that their letters not go outside the lines. This is how I was at the beginning of our relationship. Perhaps all beginnings are like that, with a certain care taken to avoid mistakes.

But we should look at all the copybooks, at the pages following those initial ones and the words near the end. Don't most students get fed up with such refinement? Don't they forget the white spaces in their notebooks and start scrawling and scribbling here and there? Who are those students who can keep their notebooks clean all year long? Are they the people in life who can maintain relationships in the same way? Haven't we all encountered those colleagues and felt jealous of their ability to keep on at the same pace?

Was Hilda really my blank page? Did she tear off the cover of my notebook? Or is this comparison silly and absurd? Why did I go back and introduce her to all my friends? Was this my way of showing off, to tell Mohsen that women could like me too? Did I do this only after I was sure of her feelings for me so to ensure I didn't ruin my image in front of them? So they wouldn't remember and keep track of my face, that long scratch on my cheek, that scar which I felt stretching all the way down my neck and reaching my leg—a leg that can't walk at a steady pace like other people's legs. I wanted them to see me essentially as a man, a man whom a woman is in love with.

I thought of Hilda now as I did the first time I saw her—this precise memory is what tormented me, making my fingers pick up the telephone and dial her number to hear her sweet voice. But my deal with myself—namely, that I would teach her the cost of her absence—prevented me.

The last thing I expected of her was to try to break the ice between us herself. But this damn woman tricked me one night when loneliness was my only companion. She called me and talked excitedly for more than five minutes about the fragrance of the soil and the land and about the airport. She described the city with love and passion. She started telling me how she felt when she stepped down onto the soil of her homeland. Her heart had opened up to the world anew, she said, as if the place had taken her by surprise, even, stunned her. The air entered the pores of her skin and filled them as if she had no bad memories of this land.

"I thought that coming back here would reopen my old wounds, but what happened was quite the opposite. Everything seemed strange. All the images that I am encountering are positive ones that bond me to this place, as if distance was what I needed to rediscover it. It's as if I've become stronger than this place, as if I'm no longer that weak young girl who fled it. It's like we've become equals, on the same level." Hilda said this quickly and passionately. Then she finished: "Everything changes, Majd, but when you look at faces and places they seem for a second as they are. Laurice made me all the foods I love, and I think that I'm going to put on weight if things continue like this. You might not recognize me when you see me." Since my reply was short and sharp she took the opportunity to ask, "Don't you want to see me? Don't you miss me?"

"Of course I do."

"Why aren't you talking to me, then?"

"Because I am tired and I want to go back to sleep."

"OK, so good night, then, sleep tight."

"You too, good night."

The call ended. I figured the phone would keep ringing all night. I wanted her to beg me to stop being so arrogant and stubborn and try to understand her. But Hilda didn't do it. She had taken her two small feet home and planted them firmly on the ground there. My trauma didn't tempt her, or perhaps it did and she was merely waiting for me to give in so she could find a way back.

A few days before she left she said, "If I don't go back, the Virgin Mary is going to be angry at me," and she told me that Laurice, the woman who worked for her family, had informed her that the statue of the Virgin in their Mount Lebanon village was crying olive oil tears.

Hilda added that while she didn't believe in these myths, she respected her mother's call for her and other relatives to visit the village and attend Sunday mass at the Holy Savior Church there, and that she, Hilda, would oblige if for nothing else but a bit of warmth.

Hilda said she'd forgotten not only how to draw the sign of the cross on her forehead but also the taste of the Eucharist and the echo of church bells.

"Pretty soon I'll forget Arabic. Do you want me to forget Arabic?" she had asked in her last attempts to get my "blessing" for her trip before she lost her temper and accused me of being selfish. I felt immune to Hilda's crying and screaming at me that night. I decided to remain silent and stop blaming her, because she said that even if she extended her trip it would be temporary.

That night we went back to bed, and I wanted to have ferocious sex with her and totally conquer her in the process. I wanted her to come near me and massage my head with her fingers. I wanted to reject her and make her try to turn me on. I turned my back to her in bed and waited, hoping she would come near me and kiss my neck, my shoulders, and my back.

I waited for her fingers that used to long for me after every fight, her nails that would dig into my skin. When my sense of touch failed me and Hilda didn't come close to me, I marshaled my sense of sound and put it on high alert to pick up on her breathing and the distance between us. I wanted to hear her heartbeats, which might reveal her desire or at least suggest that she would approach me.

After an hour or so of straining all my senses, whether by secretly looking or deliberately touching her bum with my hand as if I were moving it unintentionally, I came up against nothingness, an emptiness with no end, more that night than ever before. When I turned toward her I found she had turned her back to me herself. I got up. I approached and stopped on the other side of the bed, the side she was on. She was asleep and there was a trace of black kohl mixed with tears on her pillow.

Hilda dozed off, crying silently. I stood like a superhuman torturer contemplating the grooves of his victims' skin. When I was tired of being evil, and fed up with contemplating the torture I could cause her, I wished I could kneel down before those gray spots on her face and ask forgiveness. But when I tried to surrender, to bend my knees out of reverence to her tears, I found myself unable to adapt my body, and I remembered something my father used to always repeat to me: "Everyone with a disability is also an oppressor."

From that night on, something in the equation changed. When I looked at Hilda, I started not to see her as my girlfriend but instead I saw in her the shadow of a Christian woman. Not out of any religious motive, but rather because I was sure that when she'd go back "over there" she'd be afraid to tell her mother that she was in love with a Palestinian, Muslim man.

Perhaps she'd feel that I was a heavy burden on her, and for a few moments she'd wish that the man she'd chosen was from her background and surroundings. Hilda fled them for me. She fled all of the entitlements her family had forced her to enjoy: to be a spoiled daddy's girl who'd never grow old. She had also fled having to live with the weapons and memories of war that, for her family, had meant political power. Wartime, the time of force.

Hilda's childhood hadn't been unhappy—indeed, the very opposite—at least by external appearances. That is to say, she was a well-protected girl, the youngest of her siblings and the most spoiled one at home. This combination could have made her a superficial woman or, at the least, an indifferent young woman who didn't want to leave her family's cocoon.

But for her, as she always used to say, the caterpillar doesn't turn into a butterfly until it spins its cocoon and goes inside. The life of butterflies is more difficult because they are exposed to dust and storms; they fly and traverse long distances to discover the world.

Her parents would find it easier to stay inside their cocoon, for her to marry a man of the same confession and stay under their wing, but she didn't want to. She told them that when she was praying with her friends at school, she would always think about the sentence in the Lord's Prayer, "Lead us not into temptation." This expression in particular is what led her to ask her mother, repeatedly, about those temptations that should be avoided.

At night, before closing her eyes, Hilda used to think a lot about the things she prayed to Allah to spare her from. Did she find any answers? No. She liked the idea of knowing all the sins so that she could understand what she had been atoning for throughout her life, so that her atonement could be made flesh.

-6-

Mount Lebanon, 1982

"Hilda, why aren't you saying the act of contrition with us? I want to hear you repeat after me, 'Oh my God, I am heartily sorry for having offended Thee.'"

"Oh my God, I am heartily sorry for having offended Thee."

"And I detest all my sins because of Thy just punishments."

"And I detest all my sins because of Thy just punishments."

"Why aren't you saying the prayer in a louder voice, and finishing the act of contrition alone. Have you memorized it? And I detest all my sins because of Thy just punishments, but most of all because I have offended Thee my God."

That day, Hilda repeated the act of contrition crying, but she finished the prayer to the end. *Soeur* Jacqueline kept her in the classroom, after religion lessons, and started talking to her about repentance, about the importance of demonstrating virtue and keeping away from vice.

She told her about the sanctity of the Holy Virgin, who conceived without being defiled, but she didn't ask Hilda why she had been crying. Hilda told the sister that day that she loved God, that she didn't want to incite his wrath, and that she was afraid that he didn't love her. But *Soeur* Jacqueline assured her that our Mother Mary would intercede with God on her behalf.

Hilda was eleven years old at the time and one of her friends lived in the student residences at the school, which had a section for girls who were living in the convent.

Her friend Patricia had informed her that the nuns were stingy in feeding the girls, and Hilda dared to ask the sister if God would forgive them for that. *Soeur* Jacqueline questioned Hilda until she admitted that Patricia was the one who told her.

The next day, Patricia didn't come and play or talk to Hilda. Her friends informed her that the girl had gotten a harsh punishment from the nuns: they had forced her to recite the act of contrition fifty times for everyone to hear. Patricia stood at the edge of the playground shooting Hilda angry looks full of blame before turning her back and completely shunning her.

This pained Hilda a great deal. She hadn't meant to cause her friend any harm. "Oh my God, I am heartily sorry for having offended Thee...." Hilda knelt down in front of the window of her room praying after she came home from school, repeating the act of contrition, hoping Patricia would talk to her the following day. But she didn't.

The opposite happened. In fact, over the course of that school term Patricia unleashed her open hostility onto her and moved on to other friends. Hilda felt completely shunned by the group.

She started trying to recite different prayers each day—once to the Virgin, once to Jesus, once to God—but none of her entreaties had the intended result. She put a cassette into her tape player and tried to learn by heart the hymn *Under Your Protection*, figuring that this would perhaps be a point in her favor. In fact Hilda encouraged Patricia to help her.

"Under your protection, I take refuge, oh Mary. Don't refuse our requests when we call on you...." Hilda stopped the tape and went back and played it again until she memorized the first line. The next day she was whispering to herself, "Oh pride of mirrors, best of humankind, sea of gifts in this world passed."

Hilda went back home angry when nothing changed in the way her girlfriends were treating her. She played the tape and noticed that she'd been singing, "pride of mirrors," but the hymn went, "pride of innocence," which rhymed in Arabic. So this was why the Virgin Mary wasn't answering her prayers, she figured. Hilda cried herself to sleep.

In the second term, on Laurice's advice, Hilda decided to write a letter to her friend with lots of hearts drawn on it. She wrote that she loved her and prayed every night for her to forgive her. Indeed, soon the two friends reconciled, and Hilda regained her standing in the group. She even became more a part of the group of girls who were troublemakers, and a tendency emerged from inside her to break rules and provoke the nuns' wrath.

From the time of the incident, Hilda had a recurring dream for more than a month in which *Soeur* Jacqueline locked her in the school basement and would visit her each morning, giving her a small loaf of bread and jam or else some sesame halava that Patricia had told her about.

In this dream, the tall nun in her dark blue habit would shoot accusatory stares at Hilda, as if she had committed a sin that couldn't be forgiven, a sin the nun wanted Hilda to never be free of as long as she lived.

Even later in life, once Hilda was able to recognize this aspect of her childhood as extended psychological torture, she felt as if she was carrying around a nonexistent sin, one she'd already asked God to forgive her for.

Hilda also used to believe that she was carrying the sin of the war, and that the many weapons in their house were some kind of divine punishment. Tall men came to their house and would sit with her father and Uncle George. Her father used to ask her to stay in her room, and he would call her mother so he could tell her to not let her go out. But she used to look at them secretly through the peephole, see them exhaling their cigarette smoke nervously, and listen to the sounds of their guns. One day her father brought one of the wounded people home—his friend Antoine. "They took his weapon, we reached him when he was at his last breath," he told Hilda's mother, whom Hilda watched transform into a nurse in seconds. "Stay with him, I need to go." Her mother tended to the wound Antoine had taken in his chest and was bleeding from. They didn't have anyone working in the house at the time, so Hilda's mother was forced to make use of Hilda to bring her cloth and things from the cupboard, where the family kept medicines and first-aid supplies.

Hilda used to look fearfully at the wounded and was invariably on the verge of tears when doing so, but her mother always calmed her down. She would talk to the person while cleaning his wound, cursing the person who did it. "Curse the Palestinians and their fathers who brought them to this country and those who let them do this to our country."

Hilda would say, "Oh Jesus, Oh Mary," more than twenty times in the space of less than five minutes. She just wanted to cry, because she didn't understand what was going on. She was afraid for her mother too, as if bleeding were something you could catch. But her mother nursed all the patients and remained near them. She wasn't used to falling asleep on the sofa, but she did.

Hilda hadn't attributed such strength to her mother, and had thought her incapable of taking control of things alone—until that first night.

When Hilda told me about this incident, I tried to imagine the wounded Antoine's features, asking myself if he was wearing military fatigues that day and who shot him. I was listening to the story of a wounded man not as an enemy but simply a human being. No, I can't see him as an ordinary human being, only a combatant. I wasn't sympathetic to him because I knew that if I had been in that room twenty years ago I would have wished for his death.

None of this deterred me from listening to the story eagerly. At a certain point I felt happy because Antoine and his people were suffering, too, and I was trying to joke with Hilda and tell her that I was trying to imagine her mother's reaction if she had known about our relationship.

"Can you imagine if I was in your house, and I was speaking to your mother with a Palestinian accent? She would surely collapse."

"Why does that idea make you happy?"

"It doesn't, not at all!"

"It definitely wouldn't be fun. Do you hate them?"

"Who?"

"My family.... Us...."

"No, of course not."

"Do you love them?"

"I don't know them."

"Will you be able to love them?"

"I don't know. I will try to get to know them through you. Is it required for me to love them? Am I able to love them? Perhaps. At the end of the day they aren't Israelis. I know that I love you and I want you to be me mine alone, far from everything else. This is the only thing I know."

-7-

Mount Lebanon, 2000

At the entrance to the village on the northern side of East Beirut, Hilda asked the driver—her father had sent him to take her home—to stop. She got out of the car and went to light a candle at a shrine to Our Lady the Virgin Mary. She picked a blossom from a little tree with yellow wazzal flowers and put it in a book she was carrying in her handbag that she liked because it was big and spacious.

She knew that this kind of flower gave off no fragrance, but she used to imagine it as the reflection of the sun in nature. After this, the driver cut short the last few miles to her house, and the girl ran to throw herself on her mother's lap and hug her tightly.

She heard his laughter from far off when she had sunk right into her mother's lap, and she hurried to run over to him while he was calling her, "Bella, it's as if you haven't grown any older at all!"

"It's been more than seven years, haven't you had enough of being away?"

"It was something I had to do, Dad."

"Will you stay here now?

"It's too early to determine that."

Hilda's father was speaking to her while patting her head at times, and at others, holding her around the waist. He hugged her and he went with her into her room on the ground floor of the house. Her things were as she had left them, as though she hadn't been away from this place for even a moment. A record player; sky blue, almost greenish walls; teddy bears; and a ring of light on the ceiling above her bed. One mattress atop another with many pillows, like those usually owned by rich people.

She threw herself on her first mattress and closed her eyes for a few moments. Majd was in her bed, his eyes closed, too, trying to close the gap between them to become one. Two separate beds: a man, a woman, and a dream. What he was unable to tell her was how much he loved her; what she didn't tell him is that she would feel that the place was depressing without him, that she would reach her fingers out into the air to get him and pull him toward her and she wouldn't find him.

Majd remained torn about what distance meant, what it could take away from his loved ones. He felt he was being introduced to another Hilda, and when he remembered her, he started picturing things other than what they had in common.

He pictured in his mind her village, her dreams, and her first steps; he saw her as a young girl crawling, and a teenager spying on a friend whose desk was near hers. He concentrated intensely on these details as if he wanted to be familiar with everything important to her. He opened the closet. He looked at her dance clothes that she hung carefully in a separate section and recalled how disappointed she was when he missed her university graduation ceremony.

When she came back from the ceremony, she described to him how she had floated above the ground and tamed her muscles, her thighs, her shoulders and even her fingers to let themselves give in to the music. That day she lit a cigarette from her pack and he was surprised, watching her blowing smoke. She seemed different. She wasn't smiling. She was talking to him passionately, but it wasn't just any passion but, rather, a fervor deliberately calculated to make him feel guilty because he hadn't been there.

"I still don't understand how you didn't come," she finally said while lighting another cigarette.

"I wanted to, but an urgent meeting came up at work. I didn't know you smoked."

"It's not a big deal. I only smoke sometimes."

Before going to sleep that night, she said she was always prepared to do anything for him, whatever it was, even if she was forced to give up a part of herself or make a lot of compromises. She also informed him that she had started to call everything into question: if she loved him more than she should, if she was rushing things, or if she was lost in fantasies about great love stories. Then she cried. She kept on crying hysterically and cursing the whole business of living abroad until she fell asleep.

A part of him understood what the girl was saying, and he knew he should have been in the theater following her eyes while she danced. But another part of him couldn't explain these exaggerated reactions that happened sometimes.

That night, between the fear of losing her and the desire to alleviate the weight of her grief, all he could do was to make up an excuse for missing her ceremony. Before she let herself fall asleep, he sat near her on the edge of the bed and bent down to kiss the last of her tears, telling her that he'd had a terrible pain in his leg that had prevented him from going.

He claimed that he had in fact been heading out the door when he almost collapsed on the floor. So he leaned his body against the wall and waited a few minutes before being able to reach the sofa. He said he'd hoped to be there. He could imagine her floating off the ground, flying above it, and he saw himself flying along with her, holding her hand and wandering together, as if he had never been unable to control his leg.

Hilda started crying again, not out of anger this time but out of sadness. Affected by this, Majd's anxiety eased the situation. As she slept, he whispered the last part of the lie to her, the real part, that he had almost fallen down and hadn't been brave enough to bear watching her fly when he was stuck on this cursed earth. He told her he'd actually sat down on the sofa and that defeat was what pushed him there. He kept dreaming about her throughout the duration of her show, listening to the same music she was dancing to at the time. He told her this only when he knew that she couldn't hear him anymore. "The Last Minute," was the name of her show. "At the last minute"—so she told him while applying light blue eye shadow in a circle on her eyelids, and then eyeliner below, before going to her show's final dress rehearsal—"life turns everything upside down. The last minute summarizes everything because it determines and creates memories. Either you oust everything that came before it or decide that you will be an extension of it." She kissed him passionately and bit his lower lip flirtatiously before leaving.

He was sitting alone, imagining her body on stage. Rising and falling as if calling out to him. Every movement she made excited him. It took the scar off his face and threw away the crutch he used to walk. As if he were near her there and she were rising up there on his behalf. The theater's red and yellow played around her body, which passionately tore him to pieces. Then the lights were projected onto her face. She lifted her head up to show her neck to the crowd, open, fresh, begging to be kissed. Then she turned her head forward, in a movement synchronized with her shoulders. She looked like a woman kicking her lovers out and putting her head on a guillotine. She was there. Light. One with herself. Self-contained like a piece of art. It wasn't important in those moments if he possessed this piece of art. Its beauty was enough. But the moment he reached out his hand to capture it, he awoke from the serenity of the mirage. He was angry, but it was enough for him to curl up his fingers into a fist and punch the wall.

For him, this dream was more bearable than reality—to sit and see her like a mirage flying on the wooden stage and then throwing himself into the show as the dance partner he longed to be, not a nobody who just sat and watched.

-8-

Sabra and Shatila Refugee Camp, 1980

"What do you want to be when you grow up, Majd?"

"I want to be a pilot."

"Why?"

"To fly up and see things from above."

"Aren't you afraid you might fall someday?"

"No, I want to draw white lines in the sky like those you see behind airplanes."

"But then you'll spend most of your time away from us, traveling and never settled."

"I want to visit God's house up there. Could I do that?"

"I don't know, son."

"You always say that he is looking down on us from up there. I want to visit him."

"But I actually meant that he is further away than that."

"I want to fly and see him."

"You don't want to be a doctor, for example? Or an engineer or a teacher like your father?"

"No, Mama, I want to fly."

"Let's see if you can fly into my lap right now, come on. Climb up, come on, come!"

She laughed a lot, tickling me and kissing me on my belly while I turned my face toward the ground. She was threatening to throw me and, laughing, I said no, no, then she turned me on my back again and moved her mouth toward my shoulders, chest and belly saying, "I'm gonna eat you, let's see if you can run away now. You're my dinner tonight!"

I was screaming then laughing and we both threw ourselves onto the mattress overcome by laughter. Afterward, she pointed at the clock to let me know that my bedtime had come. After I wiggled around in my place sullenly, she would put such a stern look on her face that I knew I had to surrender.

Despite our modest circumstances, I was a carefree child before the Lebanese Civil War started. I was in a better situation than most of the children in the camp, who didn't even have decent basic living conditions. My father was an Arabic language teacher in one of the UNRWA schools, near the Shatila camp. Well dressed, nicely turned out, and mild mannered, he always wore a black and white *keffiyeh* after the Palestinian revolution gathered in our camps, though he often wore it with a suit and a necktie.

He used to combine tradition and modernity, even in his external appearance. With great pride, my mother and I gave him his nickname, "the Professor." She, "the Professor's wife," was a destination for the women of the camp, who would ask her to negotiate with her husband to give private lessons to their children or to try to intervene on their behalf with the PLO office so they could get scholarships to complete their education in the Soviet Union. My mother always promised her friends, "With God's blessing, we'll do what we can."

In the evening hours, after he'd come back home and had a bit of a rest, she would bring him a paper with the requests of the women and the names of their children. She'd tell him the history of each family and their tragedy: Abu Abdo had fallen for the fourth time on the way to the bathroom in their tiny house because he banged his head into the ladder leading to the top floor, which used to be a little attic but had become his grandchildren's room, and he tripped on the edge leading to the toilet. It was the fourth time this sixty-something-year-old man had fallen. His only son had joined the fedayeen and was no longer able to support him, his wife, and his young grandchildren. Umm Ismail wanted to replace the tin roof of the house with concrete. She cursed the UNRWA to my mother, informing her that PLO representatives had come twice to take pictures of the house but had never come back to fix it. "They won't come. If they come now, I'll throw them out," she told her. "OK, ma'am. I'll make you the camp's mayor," my father told her while taking off his jacket. "History books aren't as accurate as you are."

"No mayor, no nothing. We all have the same problems. Our pain is the same. We have only each other," she replied. This was the conclusion she had drawn since her displacement, that tragedy gathers people together, that only poor people support each other in adversity, as if one person's skin merges with another's and becomes one set of clothes, nourishment, and even beds if need be.

She used to always say that this solidarity between children of the homeland in diaspora was what allowed them to be steadfast through their displacement. She criticized rich Palestinians who abandoned their countrymen and didn't ever try to reach out to them with a helping hand. "For what reason? What would it hurt them to reach out?" she used to say while listing off the names of rich Palestinian relatives, none of whom I can still recall today. "It's as if they're not even like us at all."

My mother was also young when she came to Lebanon from Abu Sinan, her Palestinian village. She used to always say that she thought when she was a child that she would go back home—sooner or later—and that she didn't understand the meaning of occupation. She believed that what was happening was something temporary, and that, as in children's stories, the people of the village would triumph over evil and go back to their land—and who knows, perhaps she would even marry a prince.

After I grew up and became an adult, my mother started to always be sarcastic about the name of her village, as if she were reproaching the land for not daring to show its teeth and submitting to its occupier. "Why did they name it Abu Sinan? It never bared its teeth, they should have called it something else," she used to say, and my father would laugh, and then he researched the origin of this name to tell her its story.

But my mother passed away before knowing why her village was called Abu Sinan. She didn't live to see any teeth except those of oppression, hatred, death, and homelessness. As if life wanted her to submit to this logic of force and for her to pass down to me, her son, weighty feelings of hopelessness, and the law of the jungle where survival is for the fittest—those people who know how to invent real weapons, not only those bestowed upon us in fictitious competitions. It's as if life wanted to tell me that I would become a king when I stood in front of the window on the ninety-ninth floor, up on top, this is my only restitution for everything I've lost and my impregnable fortress, which no one can destroy. The only high place I ever reached was the roof of the refugee camp. My mother called out to me from below, shouting and threatening to smack me with her shoe, after she despaired of me ever coming down.

"Come down, naughty boy!"

"Leave me alone, Yamma, I want to see the sun."

"I'll tell your father when he comes home."

The roof was an outlet that allowed me to breathe in air with a different scent, to see the extent of the inhabited buildings stretched out before me and be stung by light that could hardly find its way into the camp, which was surrounded by cramped buildings, garbage piled up in alleyways, and moisture from laundry which women hung out on random lines. I didn't hear my mother's voice no matter how loud her shouting and screaming to our neighbor Wedad or Abu Mahmoud the grocer that they should come and see: "The boy won't be satisfied until he's fallen off the roof!"

"I'm telling you, come down, sweetie. Look, come down, you rascal."

"Leave me alone, Yamma, I want to see the sun."

-9-

I came to America about two years after the massacre, after my father had managed to buy tickets for his and my trip, because he had some relatives there. After my mother's death, which he refused to believe, he gave up the fighting he'd begun after being promoted from professor to fedayee. He was in a state of confusion. He didn't know if he had to give up the nickname "Professor" so he could engage in the armed struggle and join the Fatah movement.

My mother was angry. What would transform him—who couldn't even step on an ant his whole life—into a fighter? Posing him this question, she would tell him that fighting was a craft that needed skills and intensive training that he didn't have. "Think about what would happen if everyone who carried a gun became a fighter. This isn't your thing, man." But he was insistent.

There was a different light in his eyes, not the one we knew. It was one of neither victory nor hope, but rather a spark of sadness that appears in the eyes of people suffering from life, when it throws some kind of test at them. Despite his kind features, my father had a strong constitution. When he wore an olive-green military uniform for the first time, with a *keffiyeh*, he seemed to us a totally different man. It seemed like a militant inside him had split open his suit, like his muscles had suddenly grown larger and his voice had become coarser.

My mother was asking him what he would tell his students when they saw him looking like this and if they would now call him something other than "Professor." But he looked straight into her eyes and told her that people would love him more now, that they would still call him "Professor" because they were used to it. "People love power, they don't like weakness. Aren't you like that?" She nodded, surrendering in agreement, but kept on questioning him.

She tried to make him feel guilty, saying the students wouldn't quickly get used to another teacher, but he ignored her. In response to her insistence, he looked her in the eyes and told her that the game of occupation is grim, that it just about kills off the very last bit of hope for a life of justice in a person. He said that the ability of people expelled from their land—voluntarily or forcibly—to turn into fierce fighters wasn't a desire for devastation, but because devastation had happened and had grown up deep inside them.

"In such times, if I didn't carry a weapon I wouldn't be a Palestinian," he told her as if fighting for him had become a question of identity, not of choice. It was not a challenge or merely an expression of anger, but more than that—as if, for a moment, death didn't exist. He spoke and she listened, knowing full well the heartbreak in his voice; a tendon was pulling on another tendon to keep his throat together, frightened tendons hugging each other under the skin using voices, screaming, and moaning as a shelter.

She knew this tone well; it had the same rattle in it that she remembered as their displacement and fear. She knew the meaning of your soul escaping from your body through the throat, and then trying to return in panic. When his voice seemed choked up and its tendons were all like this, she surrendered to the status quo, holding his hand tightly to let him know that she completely understood what he was feeling and saying.

She stroked his face with her hand and didn't cry, as if she herself were also being brave. She thought about how many displaced and homeless people there were in the world stuck in their situations like she was, and how many men found themselves unable to be fighters—only to become nationalists and patriots, even if that meant marching quickly toward their final resting places.

Slowly, when the women of the camp started talking about the courage of my father, the Professor, whom no one had expected to be so brave, she gave to the inevitable, and the idea that she would be the wife of a powerful fighter calmed her down. It was as if he suddenly transformed into what was missing from her village, "Abu Sinan," gnashing his teeth in preparation to go back into battle.

With time, his army uniform and *keffiyeh* transformed into a source of security for us as if they were a good enough reason for him to suddenly come and go. Despite the difficulties of distance and life without him in this period, rarely did my mother complain about him; instead she always looked at him with awe, reverence, and love. She boasted about him like religious people do about their ideological legacies and their holy places.

He loved her, too, and he remembered her after she passed away; he would describe her as a symbol of purity, chastity, and virtue. A few months before he died, he confessed to me too that he felt as if he were touching her for the first time every time he was with her.

"She would put on those things that women do just for me—lace and satin, and she'd spray perfume on the bed—but she always maintained that shyness that makes you feel like you are on virgin land where no creature had ever set foot. She was a virgin every time. Her tender freshness erased any old signs of me from her body and she wore an entirely new skin."

When my father recounted this to me, when I became a young man, I was surprised he could be so bold. I was confused. Was this also one of his fabrications? Had distance from her made her seem like a dream? Was his inability to touch her now for real what made his image of her so beautiful and intimate? Was what my mother represented to him—"A virgin every time, as though you are stepping on untouched land"—what in fact put him into a state of denial about her death?

My father said he didn't ever feel he was a hero on the ground during any battle, as much as he did feel like a hero when she looked at him; therefore feelings of guilt about her death mounted inside him—as if he had been late in coming to her rescue or had left her when she needed him most. The sentence, "Take the boy and go," was enough to make me feel guilty as well.

Was I the reason she was left to face this bleak fate? How could this be if I preferred not to live than to live without her? Was my leg injury my eternal burden because

I was the cause of her death? Was I really the reason? Why didn't my father ever deal with me as if I'd made him lose his wife? Is he that mature or did his fatherly feelings overpower blame?

I always used to think about what would have happened if my leg hadn't been injured and if my father hadn't carried me far away. Would we have all died together like a cousin of his once said, or was there some hope we could have saved her? Perhaps a man like me, from a certain place where miracles happened, through reaching the top of my profession, should no longer be allowed to believe in the myth that God punishes us physically for our sins and transgressions.

I always thought of Hilda and I imagined her reciting the act of contrition, asking myself: Do I have to also pray to God and tell him, "I am sorry"? Sorry because some enemy caused my leg injury and pushed my father and me far away from the refugee camp, so my mother died alone—all because of me.

Would I be forgiven if I read out the act of contrition like Hilda did or if my disability washed my face with tears? Would all of this go away if I told God I was a sinner? Was this my perpetual attempt to exhaust my painful leg? Do I try to punish it because I haven't forgiven myself for what happened on that fateful day?

The two years preceding our coming to America were by far the most difficult. Returning to the memory of death, and stepping on dead bodies, one of which might be your mother, is the most difficult thing I have ever experienced. Coming back to the camp broken, as if you knew that you were a stranger there, no longer able to convince yourself that it could ever be even a temporary refuge for you. These were the feelings of most of the people who survived the massacre at Sabra and Shatila: we might die at any moment and no one would come to our rescue.

At the time, my father also lost his zeal for fighting. When he walked it was as if he were dragging disappointment behind him, as if he'd become an old man in one day. His age doubled overnight.

He cast off his nickname, "Professor," as well as his military garb and became obsessed with looking after me, as if I were the only booty left to him in this world—a spoil of war that, perhaps, he wouldn't have to relinquish.

I recall him dressing the wound on my face regularly, cleaning it with disinfectant, and helping me walk on one leg. He would stand at the other end of the house and encourage me to come to him, smiling from a distance and opening his arms to me.

At the time, feeling like a one-year-old toddler, I summoned up a newborn's desire to embrace life, and so I took a step forward. The foyer seemed like a long, unending tunnel I had to cross to reach his arms. My father's goodness made me unable to even think about increasing his grief. I would have done anything to please him, to see him smile a little.

Some evenings, some of his friends would visit; they would gather in the living room on a mattress on the floor. I would make tea and take sit with them to hear what they were talking about. Some of them were angry and vicious, others frustrated and in pain.

Their conversation revolved around the latest political and military developments, and I listened to what they were saying without understanding much. The truth is that my father was fairly indifferent about what would happen. His only obsession was to get me to another country. He told his friends that he discovered that what existed here, between the Christian militias and the Arab leadership, went well beyond the Zionist hatred for Palestinians.

Echoing my mother's words, he said that, because we were weak, no one would lend a helping hand to our people. He said that the contempt he experienced here from those people who were supposed to be Arabs like him went beyond the hatred of the Israelis. Becoming like someone who considers that any fighting outside the homeland is futile, he always said that if his people had stayed in Kafr Yasif and only left as lifeless corpses, it would have been better than the humiliation its people were living with today.

"It turns out that now we escaped to fight outside our lands, like those people who till someone else's soil." These were his words as he cautioned all those around him that there is more to come, that death would continue to haunt the Palestinians, like curses unjustly haunt some people.

To be Palestinian, either you forget your roots and deny your origins in order to advance in life, or you remain a bullet in the barrel of a rifle waiting to be fired in some direction, hostile to life, because it plundered your birthplace and forced you to invent a homeland.

To be Palestinian, especially in wartime, is to deny yourself your right to life, to wear sorrow as a skin, and not lose the love of your country. To be Palestinian is to forget laughter and be committed to feelings of injustice and victimization, even if always remaining one of the Kharijites.

It is to be born in a shelter or a refugee camp and see everyone looking at you with pity or disgust, the majority considering you a burden. It's to wait for international aid and UNRWA donations, to fear having children—like Muhammad, my Auntie Zahra's son in the camp. Because he knows how hard it would be for his child to grow up Palestinian.

But in one of the stages of my life, because I am my father's son—that man who chose the trajectory of my life, taking me far from death—I had to choose to be a different kind of Palestinian, someone determined with all his will to go beyond this definition, defy reality, and forget for a moment what the homeland is. The homeland he has never been to.

After I came to New York with my father, as a teenager with a damaged leg, it seemed to me that perhaps there was hope here that rose up like skyscrapers. This land felt like the opportunity for me to jump on one foot, deserving a fresh start that would perhaps be better.

I was well aware of the opportunity my father secured for us and I wanted to seize it fully. All the advantages and disadvantages of that trip were increasingly evident to me when I got in touch with some of my relatives in the camp and after I started receiving letters from my cousin Muhammad.

This relationship that grew up late between us reminded me of the people of my homeland and their suffering. Muhammad used to write long emails whose abundant typos always seemed to me a sign of his troubles. It is as if his defeat were reflected in the letters in front of me, letters faltering on the screen, chasing each other like pain racing out into the open from which to express itself. He used to write from an Internet café his Lebanese friend had opened at the edge of the camp. He passed most of his free time there helping his friend a little while going online when he could.

Muhammad would describe the dirt at the edges of the Sabra and Shatila refugee camp. He would send me pictures and ask me to send him pictures of America, asking me how life was here. He would describe the passersby inside the camp as if they were ghosts.

"You should see the tangled mess of electric wires. This tiny community we live in is getting more and more cramped by the day. Believe me, the small camp that was here and that our ancestors thought would be temporary has become detached buildings, narrow camp alleyways, and houses without balconies. This is not our tragedy, my friend. The tragedy is that day by day we lose hope of ever escaping here," he said in one of his letters.

Muhammad wrote at length about the water leaking through the roofs and of the alleys the rain submerged so much that people living in the camp could swim in them. As for the jumbled-up wires, they resembled a coercive embrace that no doubt one day would end in an explosion. The lines of his letters contained visible sarcasm together with a despair that pleads for some hope. In my responses, I used to reassure him patiently and try to minimize things by convincing him that life was the same everywhere.

But whenever I stood on my office balcony in that tall building and imagined the camp and its inhabitants, I could almost hear the rain running down off the roof. Sometimes I could reach my hand out to touch the tangled electric wires or pick up a child, lift him out of there, and take him far away.

Whenever I read Muhammad's letters, which always repeated his desire to marry and have children, as he was now more than thirty-five years old, I would ask myself if this really was a desire to experience fatherhood or simply a desire for a normal life and nothing more? Most Palestinians get married and have children. Why didn't he dare do it?

I also had this desire, but was afraid of it because of my disability. I was afraid to not be able to carry my son because one of my hands would be holding my crutch. I was afraid to not be able to jump around with my child in the park and I imagined that if I had gotten married and my wife would have given birth, my feelings of failure toward my son would have eaten away at me, like similar feelings did at Muhammad. I suppressed this fire inside me, and I wasn't able to encourage Muhammad to marry and have children with the girl he loved whom he always wrote about in his letters.

He used to say that he was afraid of the day when another man would come, a competent and well-off man who would to steal her from him, right under his eyes, because that other man could provide her with a good living. I also used be in that same incomplete state of love, even in the throes of my infatuation with Hilda. In fear of losing her, I would see her slipping between my fingers and our passionate love turning into a mere illusion. Muhammad was expecting to see his girlfriend's window locked one day, and his eyes remained fixed on her. He was unable to leave the camp for fear of being away from her.

She lived on the edge of the camp, in the Lebanese part. She was poor, like him, and he loved her but her family would not accept his request to marry her. He asked the mothers of his Lebanese friends if they would accept having their daughters marry someone like him. Some of them politely said they would and others openly said they would refuse. "Why do you want to marry a Lebanese woman?" one of them said. "Marry a Palestinian." So he told her that his girlfriend was Lebanese. "But love goes the same way it comes," she said. "It will pass."

All doors seemed firmly shut in Muhammad's face. Where could he find money and decent work opportunities? "I want her, I don't want anyone else. So what if I'm Palestinian? Who cares?" This is what he would tell his mother, who tried to persuade him to give up on this love story when she saw him angry or hurt. "Leave me alone, Yamma!"

Muhammad couldn't leave and pursue work elsewhere, because he knew that he would return to find her married to someone else. Preempting the locked window was an obsession of his, just like my fear about Hilda's return to Beirut was for me.

This preempting of unhappy endings left all of us defeated, as if our bodies were stuck to the ground without any glue being there, or anything else specific that forced us to stay there like that. I could never tell my cousin to leave and try to find some kind of opportunity and come back hoping the window that he believed doomed to be locked would stay open.

How could I ask him this? Me, someone who couldn't even watch Hilda dance fearing the sight of her body floating above the ground, suspended in mid-air. I never told him that stuck bodies, which try to rise up but then fall back down again, survive better than body parts that just flounder around in place. In every letter, I was expecting Muhammad to tell me something different. I was expecting some courage and some hope from him, as I was from myself.

Part Two

-I-

New York, 2000

What I don't understand about myself is the contradiction between my many fears and the victories I've achieved, the image of a successful man that swept away my tragedy and my insistence on not being subjected to plastic surgery for the scar on my face. I wasn't ugly. Brown skin, hazel eyes, somewhat coarse but not unkempt hair. And my height gave me a physical coordination that eased my awkward gait.

At the beginning of my professional journey, I neglected my outward appearance, but Hilda coming into my life changed this too. She started buying my clothes and color-coordinating them. I never dared to wear colored sports shoes before I met her but she encouraged me. The first time I put on these light blue shoes, I kept staring in the mirror and laughing. Would I go out like this? I asked myself. I laughed even more and remembered Salma's story. She was the daughter of our neighbor in the camp. When her mother bought her new shoes for Eid al-Adha, she put them in the freezer to preserve them so they would stay new. Her mother came the next day and laughed. She told the story to my mother in a voice interrupted by giggling, faltering over letters and words. They were white sandals with flowered straps. The girl carried them with her when she went with her mother on visits, scared they'd be stolen. She put the box on her lap and every other second looked inside to check that they were still there.

I kept looking at the new gray sports shoes and their wide blue stripes with a satisfied smile. Despite how strange this all was, the idea was seductive: my feet had become different. I was used to suits, neckties, and prescription glasses that I rarely took off. The colorful sports shoes seemed like something worn by those Americans who were happy with their lives.

There were contradictions in my outward appearance between a man who was marked by war and displacement and the stylish clothes he wore. It was as if on the one side I myself were a brilliant shiny coin, and when you turned it over, the other side was marked by a giant gash. When any of the workers at the video game development company I worked at came into my office, I would always be standing in front of the window, my back to the door. As soon as I turned around, my visitor's face would betray surprise, and the person would be nervous for a few minutes before reaching out a hand to say hello.

I used to see that very same expression on everyone's face: people trying to resist looking at the repulsive scar on my face. I would then balance my hand on the wall for the few steps that would take me to my desk, so I didn't need to carry my cane in that small space. The visitor would then wake from the shock of the scar to focus on my limp, and the hushed questioning would increase.

Sometimes visitors wouldn't ask what happened to me, but curious people wouldn't leave it alone. I would invent stories, including one that I fell off the balcony at my grandfather's house when I was young, and another that I fell off a motorbike and my face was cut on a broken glass bottle on the ground. I was well-versed in lying, and I did it for fun. Other times, when I was in a bleak mood, I would go further and talk about the massacre—how the perpetrators were never held accountable, and then plunge into a long monologue about war and its tragedies until my visitor was bored and uncomfortable.

"That's terrible!"

"Did all that happen to you?"

The sentences that I heard from Americans made it seem like they were living on another planet, they didn't know that things like this really happened to us, the Arabs.

"You are so brave!"

I would smile and they would press my hand tightly and I would try to seem moved by their emotions. If I had not been so well-skilled in my profession and familiar with the world of technology, my clients wouldn't have so easily felt comfortable with me after sitting together for such a short time. I always succeeded in giving priority to my image as a successful businessman despite my physical disability. Perhaps because of this I wanted them both to intersect, so I could preserve my distinctiveness, or in order not to deceive people, for them to know me as I was, in my old skin, not skin fabricated in a medical clinic.

The problem wasn't ever how I appeared to strangers or even people close to me, but how I trained myself to bridge this gap between myself and other people. The problem wasn't my Palestinianness or my desire to escape it at times, but rather coming to terms with those feelings of alienation from a place I don't know and where I have no memories, from a land that inhabits me that I have never stepped foot on.

Perhaps keeping my scar was a way to say I am from there, from that undefined place. It's a place whose area grows more constricted and decreases every day. Perhaps, in this way, someday it will unjustly become extinct. It was that utopian place in which all beautiful meanings turned into pain, as if it explained both the lack of logic and the actual truth. The painful, beautiful, blunt truth in its sincerity. It was an admission of life and its tragedies.

Similarly the tension in my relationship with Hilda was an admission of the difficulty of people of different genders coming together harmoniously to the point that they became unified in body and soul. Our physical relationship was like a yearning to come together, a yearning that was difficult to achieve.

I wasn't that flexible guy who was able to always control the movements of his body, and I had to train them to get used to my disability. When I met her, I used take her in my arms and keep her there so I could feel that she had started to crumble between my fingers, which moved in that space between her breasts and buttocks, waiting for her to become weak and submissive so I could tell her how she should move in harmony with my body.

I felt her belly lying on me while I was stretched out under her, asking her to look at herself in the mirror and see how her face had become shiny and transparent, while she was in this position. I used to see embarrassment trying to overcome itself. I would ask her afterward to look right in my eyes and kiss me as if she had just discovered herself and she wanted to share her mouth with me.

But when Hilda started to know everything, how to move and where to touch me, despite the pleasure I felt, I started fearing she would want more from me. Even though I was afraid that she wouldn't help me with my leg, I hoped in fact that she would keep not knowing how—so I could remain the teacher, she the pupil discovering the world through me. But then she seemed to mature all at once, that kind of maturity there's no going back from, indeed you only get more and more mature. She became like America, an unsolved mystery.

Every time I went back home and didn't find her, I was increasingly convinced she would never return. She managed to leave, and a person who has this ability doesn't turn back. I used to look at her pictures, as if this was all that remained of her, as if the scent of her skin was still lingering in all the corners of the house but would never fill it with its fragrance again. On one of those nights, when I was lost thinking about Hilda, an American friend of mine, Marianne, came to my place, knocking on my door like a madwoman.

I opened it and she sat down on the sofa. She stayed silent for a few minutes and then burst into tears. She held onto a small pillow from the edge of the sofa and put it between her teeth and bore down on it, squeezing it in her hands. She was biting this pillow with all the force and anger she had in her, but it wasn't enough.

She threw herself down and put her face on my shoulder, and then started looking at her hands covered in tears as if they were strange to her. I didn't know what to do and I didn't come near to wipe away her tears. I knew well how grief can make you have to bite pillows and how burdensome pain can be if you find no escape but this basic, primitive gesture.

She carried on by saying that she was not a woman, that she no longer felt like a woman. She put her hand on her breasts and asked me to look at them, at her skin where wrinkles had started to appear. "It's a lost life, timeless and endless. They say that femininity is having a sexy body, big breasts and full lips: they can go to hell. I have all of these things, but I don't feel that I'm a woman. Do you know? I look at your body and sometimes I am jealous of you because it's incomplete. It seems to me that you are able to feel it more, appreciate it. Often we become more aware of what we've lost. I lie down in bed with some guy, I want him in those moments to be that missing part of my body that I need, so I can completely be that image of a woman, but I find myself distant. I don't feel natural anymore, I can't hold someone in my arms and feel safe and relaxed. I feel panicked, that's all I feel, then I pretend to be happy until I find some excuse to leave."

She was quiet for a bit, and then said, "Look at my face and tell me: What do you see? Do you see a happy woman?"

"I see a beautiful woman," I replied.

"What beauty is there in me now?"

"You aren't trying to seem beautiful. That is truly beauty."

I waited for her to calm down and I brought us both glasses of beer. Her hand was shaking and when she tried to lift it to her lips, it shook more. At a certain moment my fingers seemed to hesitate between touching her cheeks and not consoling her.

The hand started to move away with a mixture of cruelty, disappointment, and fear. Marianne was talking with great difficulty and asking after each sentence if I knew what she meant. She apologized for coming over, all of a sudden just like that, and repeated that she was in dire need of a friend.

I tried to alleviate her discomfort. I told her that she perhaps might find me like that some day, standing at her doorstep, waiting for her to let me in so I could fall down on the floor and start complaining. Marianne had American and Indian roots. Her features were a perfect convergence of these two civilizations—some antagonism, contradiction, and intimacy that left you confused.

She was indeed beautiful, with the kind of beauty that in some women becomes more radiant as they grow older. Hilda was like that, too, a mature fruit who was becoming tastier and more satisfying. They were both that kind of woman, who can't be stopped from living life. It's impossible to confine them merely to household and family responsibilities.

The two of them were the type who couldn't stop living even if they wanted to. Perhaps this was the biggest reason for my fear of losing Hilda: I knew that my handicap represented a kind of loss, one of the faces of death, as if I were the last pawn left in a chess game. If it made a wrong move, everything would fly away. I couldn't afford the potential cost of that move. So I stopped playing and sank into a state of inertia. It became no longer a battle with an opponent but with time, a battle that couldn't be won because it wouldn't soon destroy everyone or threaten them with force, but would make them confront it.

Time also was Marianne's enemy, but her situation was different. She wasn't escaping it, but it weighted heavily on her and was far away. Her husband had gone with the American army to the Gulf in the beginning of the nineties and disappeared after a few months, in the Battle of Khafji, when the Iraqi army advanced toward Saudi Arabia. The American army was a part of the international force that went to the region to help Kuwait against Saddam Hussein's invasion. International troops remained on the Saudi border, preparing for a confrontation. John was one of them.

Marianne wasn't politicized at the time and didn't know if she had to support her government's decision. She knew only that she didn't want to lose her husband. The time he spent away from her and his two children was painful for her. She thought it was a kind of injustice to go and fight in other people's lands. She didn't hate Arabs but she hated her government.

Marianne was an American woman who didn't like America, but at the same time she couldn't just leave. After her husband went to Kuwait, she often repeated to him in telephone calls and letters that she didn't agree with what was happening and she felt outraged that life had thrown their family into a very difficult ordeal that wasn't her fault.

She started compulsively following news reports to watch what was going on and consulting history books and political accounts as if they would show her what was left of her life. Marianne even sent a letter to the mayor of New York City and signed every petition opposing US intervention in wars around the world. From the beginning of his deployment she acted as if she knew he wouldn't come back. She expressed her outrage in her letter to the mayor, telling him that she'd discovered that there was no freedom in these glittering city lights:

> *I can't write you this letter without feeling that I am a woman bereft of choices, a woman who found herself faced with her husband's gullible enthusiasm for this rush to war. We talk about freedom all the time, and we say that we want to bring it to the world. But we—at least those of us the system is watching—know we've been deceived. All of these international resolutions, which we don't agree with, are carried out after stirring speeches about "democracy." The United States doesn't like losers or the weak but it always speaks in their name. I was imagining my husband today, standing in a line of soldiers who fired bullets without knowing why they're there. It seems to me that we aren't different than the East, where they stand behind their rulers. I want my husband back and I want my children to stop asking me where their father is. This is the only democracy that will satisfy me as an American citizen.*

After a few days, a response came from the mayor who expressed his sympathy with her feelings as a wife, but made clear that the man who was in the Gulf right now had gone there of his own volition, without being forced by state power, the American government, or any other kind of pressure.

This all happened before Marianne's husband John disappeared in the war, after months of being missing. All trace of him was lost and still was on that day she stopped by my place, after more than nine years of being missing. She couldn't know for sure if he had been killed, lost his memory, was lost himself, or was buried under the desert sand.

Her tragedy had no end. The worst misfortune became waiting, feeling that the flame that had lit up your life had transformed into a weak candle that no longer gave off light but just burned. Marianne didn't know if she was a widow or a wife; she had no answers to her children's many questions. She took them every weekend to Central Park to go out all together; sometimes they would ride in a horse carriage there or stop at lunchtime at one of the kiosks and eat a hot dog. Then they would go to the petting zoo near the 64th Street entrance and reach their little hands out to touch the animals. Rarely would she do anything without her two children, as if she needed to compensate for their father's absence. When he was first away, the older one would wake up at night crying and shouting, "I want Daddy, I want Daddy." Marianne would panic and lose her patience sometimes. She sought out a specialist to learn the best way to deal with such situations. She also learned to stay on the sidelines, to sit still and calmly, to not transfer anger onto her children, and to smile at them even in the worst moments.

Hope that her husband would return was dwindling by the day but never disappeared. Dim hope transformed into despair but never stopped. In a tiny spot in her brain she needed a dead body, or a death certificate, to be sure that it was logical if she acted as if he would never return. Without that tangible evidence of death, a person remains submerged in possibilities, refusing the end and, with it, any new beginnings.

"If only there were a body, just a body.... I have the right to a body," she told me.

All that was left of him was a handful of papers in which he narrated his daily life of waiting: how they were wearing gas masks in the extreme heat, anticipating a chemical attack. He told her that the men there were strong. They woke up early. They were subjected to strenuous training. They lined up in rows and listened to the unit commander, who lectured them about loyalty to the nation and their role in making the world a better place. He wrote:

> *Under the sun you see army divisions trading determined, powerful glances, leaving no room for fear. The sand glistens beneath their military boots, obediently. I stare into the others' eyes and listen to conversations while we are eating. One of them talks about his daughter all the time, another about his girlfriend. One of them always stays silent, so much so that we don't even know the sound of his voice. At moments, faced with our own fate, we feel weak. We feel the inevitability of our existence here as if this fate were irreversible. No one talks about the uselessness he feels when confronted by proximity to death. But, you know, at least we feel our participation in the ranks of the army is a kind of distinction. A fighter has to*

paralyze his mind and worry about the next battle so his grim wait is not so long. I know you're angry with me, but you must know that I miss you, the children, and our home. Home seems so far from here, but please believe that I will come back. I love you.

Recently, Marianne tried to retrieve the woman inside herself and act as if John weren't coming back. She was exhausted and frightened and needed to open up a new horizon in order to overcome her feelings about death. But every time she would sneak into a new boyfriend's flat, she would retreat in panic, in the middle of the night, to go back to her children, submerge herself in them, and hold their bodies close.

She told me that when a person has spent long nights alone, it later becomes difficult for them to share a bed. The idea of finding herself with a man or waking up next to him was what led her to flee—to put a limit on her feelings of fullness. Instead of seeing a man next to her, she used to see a sudden disappearance. But the desire to have a partner tortured her.

"I know I need to be with one of them, to feel that I am a woman, to laugh, to enjoy myself, but I find myself afraid and alienated from myself as if by doing this I am betraying John or making him into just a memory," she told me, expressing her fear that she was more hysterical than she should be.

"Try to build a relationship, at least to fulfill your body," I told her.

"But sex is a double-edged sword," Marianne replied. "Either it lets us feel full or we are afflicted by an emptiness beyond all emptiness. In my state, it doesn't make my body feel satiated. It anesthetizes my pain but it doesn't give me the comfort that I need."

She also said she started to worry about the impression she left on her boyfriend's spirit, when she transformed suddenly from a woman who had the right to be in love to a burden—like those women who always spoil lovely moments, whom she'd struggled her whole life to resist becoming one of.

It is always a struggle, between belonging to someone else or being satisfied with belonging to ourselves, to be complete within ourselves or turning into just parts. But Marianne's life, crowded with the responsibilities of motherhood, had been stolen from her and become unsustainable. Her tears were grief for what she didn't know and the bedroom she would never share with someone.

I also used to feel a bleak heaviness when everyone would fall asleep. I would imagine them, husbands and wives and children, and look at the side of the bed where Hilda used to sleep and not find her. I neither found a crumpled bed in the morning nor heard the clicking of another spoon as I ate.

After she calmed down, I told Marianne that she had to escape the burden of her husband's fate, that her waiting had become like little doses of poison. She needed to allow him his choices: it was enough that she loved him and loved everything they shared.

I told her that sometimes we are forced to surrender to the fact that some things will become memories, if only so those things don't destroy us. I knew very well how hard it was to live without closure. The squandered rights and dead bodies that had no one to cover them in the Sabra and Shatila massacre seemed to me as if they were still exposed, still naked, still violated. I remembered the land of the camp, which I no longer saw as made of asphalt, but of piles of dead body parts, and I thought about the land where America established itself by trampling upon the dead bodies of its indigenous peoples, who lived there first.

It was difficult for me to tell my girlfriend that the gamble of freedom was not that you risk death but, rather, love. I was overcome by hatred much of the time and it ate away at me, like a worm eating an apple and making it rotten to the core.

But she had to forget. Not to forgive her government or simply disregard her sadness about her husband, but rather in order to get herself together and to carry on with some strength. Life doesn't allow us the privilege of being weak and crying over lost love: acclimatizing to these circumstances will never be a choice but a condition of life. In the harshness of this world, pain and sadness are also a luxury that the vanquished don't have. We must forget about what we don't like, what we don't want, and make tragedy into irony so we can get out of bed in the morning. Isn't this what we do? Faced with an anger that operates inside of us, we try to convince ourselves of many things to move forward. Don't we outsmart suffering by becoming a part of it and pretending that we've overcome it? Suffering that comes from wherever and is buried inside people makes them feel as if they are small when faced with life and unable to do anything. This is what was fated for Marianne, because she was a mother and mothers can't die before their time, before they've made sure their children are safe. They can't just pass away before their time like my mother did. I woke up one night searching for her only to realize that her absence completely demolished the child's image of support and stability. The sandwiches my mother used to wrap up for me in newspaper and that I would eat—dry ones and moist ones—were never at all like her sandwiches carefully wound in plastic wrap and lined up in Tupperware boxes to keep them fresh, even if she had made them hours before. I was embarrassed to take them out of my bag when the other students had their sandwiches on French bread or had salad or butter cookies, so I would go and eat my lunch in a corner. After we moved to New York, my father enrolled me in Hamilton Heights middle school in Harlem, though at my age I should have been in high school. That was the only solution, because I wasn't able to keep up with my peers' level of English, because I had missed so much schooling after my injury. What gave me comfort was a strict and disciplined teacher who constantly stressed the importance of excelling in school, saying, "That is the only solution, and it's key for someone who's lost his country."

I used to see in Marianne that same insistence on her children studying hard. In her predicament, my friend seemed to me to have an Arab spirit. Like other Arabs, I often assert that loyalty is a characteristic that only we have, even when treason has become the rule in our societies. It was difficult for me to see her as an American, because of some label in my mind that used to make me think that foreign women couldn't have strong, warm feelings.

Whenever I heard her talking, I thought about how I—in spite of the fact that I could integrate into this Western society to some extent—was still so stereotypically Arab deep down. I couldn't stop categorizing people into foreigners and Arabs even when I tried to.

Somewhere, there is a "them" and I am always a part of "us." Even if unconsciously, I still used to see them—that is to say, non-Arab women—as concubines captured in war. This notion exists somewhere within me in all its barbarity, and yet so too does my denial of it.

Perhaps in Hilda too I used to see an attempt to avenge my displacement, an attempt to prove to the old Christian enemy—her family—that I, a Palestinian they had tried to annihilate, had now returned: through the heart of their daughter and the heart of their very home.

Perhaps one of the facets of my love for Hilda was my escape from the inferiority of my past and my victory over my pride when wandering among those killed in the war. That was the heyday of the youth I was trying to recover: that Hilda the Christian woman loved me was my sign of our worth as Palestinians. Love, not massacres.

This is what excited me the most. The instinctual, primitive side of passion. Except that I was disabled. I didn't seduce her with a complete body, but one missing something. What more than that could make a man like me feel whole? That missing part is what I will use to cleanse the shame. Isn't this enough to make ours an epic love story?

But contrary to what people believe, epics don't create love, only myths. The other side of my love for Hilda was what the scenario took from the intrigue of legend. This was the contradictory side of my hostility toward her. At the place where she stirred my heart, Hilda was not a Christian girl. It was foolish to reduce her to this, as in an epic. Hilda was a mirror I wasn't afraid to look into, a repository that carried confessions, and a smile that gave me hope for life.

In her purity and sincerity, she was all religions. She was in fact the only one true religion that doesn't try to trick you and make you feel you are being tested. The religion that doesn't try to tempt you and be a mystery you're forced to discover. She was all this and more. Therefore in most of the details of what was between us, I couldn't consider her an illusion, an epic, or revenge. This side of our relationship was just purely love.

There was always a struggle between the executioner and the victim inside of me. The only time when I felt at ease, ease and not pleasure, was when I gave up both of those roles and enjoyed our existence as loving, when I enjoyed being lovers. When she would sit on my lap and I would play with her hair, I simply loved her without remembering what I couldn't keep up with.

Marianne stayed and we talked until dawn, when she got herself together to go back and hug her children. They were her security blanket, as she always put it. She told me that night how difficult she found it to build a relationship with a man.

She felt that she was split into two halves. One was completely immersed and engaged in life's concerns and difficulties and how to overcome them. The second half was yearning to live life and collided with the first. "Perhaps that's what life is," she told me, "the attempt to escape tragedy. Perhaps life is tragedy, because it engenders hope for something better." I completely understood her, that attempt to come out of your shell and live, only to find yourself struggling with what you are meant to deal with.

Marianne didn't want to be that lost woman who didn't know anything about her husband's destiny, but she found herself in this position. Just as many people find themselves in circumstances that don't live up to their expectations. This was one side of my story, the struggle with the beginning and its consequences, the continual and pervasive desire inside me to forget where I came from, to forget a country I never knew except in my father's stories and my mother's nostalgia, to forget the experience of war that left its mark on my body, just as Marianne's marriage left her with two children as an extension of a love she wasn't sure should end.

That night she informed me as well that she was in constant contact with Hilda. I tried to hide my passion and rein in my questions about how my girlfriend was doing and whether she mentioned me in their conversations. I saw blame in my American friend's eyes for my stubbornness and insistence on punishing Hilda for having gone to Beirut.

A number of times she almost told me that I had not done right by Hilda. Though she didn't, I saw that look of blame in her eyes. She told me that Hilda was an exceptional and genuine woman, as if to affirm my unfairness toward her. I could have confessed to Marianne all the pain I felt over my distance from Hilda, told her that I saw Hilda's shadow in every corner of the house, and admitted that I was afraid that she wouldn't reciprocate this love I felt and couldn't express well enough.

I was adamant that our distance was a test, that Hilda had the choice to return if she wanted, the choice I wanted automatically, unaware that my young girlfriend perhaps needed reassurance, like me, that she was deep inside me, that place in my heart which no one could uproot her from.

I used to dream that our relationship had an end, like in a silly novel whose heroine comes back from her trip out of love that has conquered everything. What is that everything our love has conquered? My physical weakness, my inability to dance, our differences in identity, my feelings of death. I wanted love to claim a victory over all this without me having to make a huge effort to preserve it, as if I were avenging love, my right to it, and the opportunity to be happy that was once in my hands.

-2-

"Son, do you know why I brought you to America? Because all the fighting in Lebanon won't ever change anything. Don't ever think, son, that I'm not patriotic or that I'm a coward. We are Palestinian, but even if we stay in Lebanon we will become extinct. I could have been wrong when I left my land, but we are strangers there and we are strangers here in America." This is how my father summed up for me his decision to leave the camp.

He used to talk to me at length about the land and describe the village: the color of the soil, the red-tiled houses. People outside their homeland are invariably humiliated, he would tell me again and again. "They all sold us down the river.... My son.... The Arabs sold us to the Jews and we believed every day that we would return the next—a little longer and we'd return. Until now we have not returned. Your mother is there, like I told you, your mother is there." He would tell me that his people pitched tents when they left their homeland to go "over there," believing then that it would be a temporary stay until they returned to Palestine. They knew it was a catastrophe, but they didn't know what catastrophes were. They hadn't experienced this before; they couldn't imagine it clearly. They believed that the moment of displacement was the apex of their tragedy, but they learned the hard way that the future is worse and the past sometimes seems better when the present becomes bleak and the future is unknown. They lived in those tents for almost five years. They would be swept away when there were intense storms or they would drown in mud when it rained for a long time. They were finally allowed to build their camps, not one of which could be more than a kilometer and a half wide. Their population increased while the space remained the same, and so they started building vertically. They named the neighborhoods in the camp after names of their villages in Palestine: Tiberias, Ayn Zaytoon, Lubiyyeh, and Ras al-Ahmar. On the walls they wrote the distances that separated their homeland from the places they were currently in. I remember well the sign in the Shatila Camp: "Established in 1949, 92 kilometers from the Palestinian border." They tried to move their homeland with them when they went so they wouldn't lose their identity. "They didn't know that the occupation would swallow up these villages. How could they know? They were told they would return. They'd stay a little and then return."

This is how my father told it.

About five years after we came to America, before he died, he advised me about my mother, "Your only security is your mother, never forget to go back to her when things are calmer." I realized that my mother represented Palestine to him, the one he dreamed one day of returning to.

He asked me to look after the olive trees when I went back, and told me that though my mother was very sturdy she couldn't take care of them alone. For a few moments, I believed that she was there and I wanted to surrender to that dream space like he did, to throw the weight of tragedy into the hope of return, to hang images on this hope of all the loved ones we'd lost. As if the Palestinians who lived outside their homeland would come back from the dead the moment the land was liberated. As if time could be turned back decades, to before our displacement, and the story would be completed from there. As if devastation hadn't ever touched us.

But aren't these dreams unrealistic? Israel had taken hold of our lands, doing whatever it wanted. We Palestinians, where could our hope come from? From the notion of returning to lands that were shrinking every day? What miracle would it be that could destroy this evil lurking in us—we, the people whom God had forsaken in their ordeal?

How were we moved into this weak position where we now succumb to humiliating checkpoints on our own land? What is this power ensuring that you are uprooted from your own home and expelled from it, while it sits on the world's throne? Is this what evil does? Is this revenge for the massacres experienced by the Jews, or will the story be flipped around one day, and will we Palestinians somehow become the oppressors? Will we take revenge on Israel by oppressing a weaker people ourselves when life's balance of power is turned upside down?

Under the New York sky, even if I am using my cane as I walk through the streets, feelings of freedom sometimes overwhelm me. I walk at a slow, unhurried pace, and for a few moments absolute weightlessness envelops me: I am this nobody, a stranger, a transient on an anonymous path no one knows a thing about.

Even my identity stops being a burden. I see people busy with their daily concerns, details of their lives far removed from issues and causes: ordinary people of all nationalities, one of them dragging a little suitcase, another holding a map and looking at it to find the destination.

Another man is carrying a small bag, headed for work as the sun rises the same over everyone. The weird thing is that what makes this place beautiful also makes it agonizing: I always remain a stranger. I'm not in the camp, where pretty much everyone knows everyone else. But isn't it taken for granted that Palestinians would all know each other in this overcrowded spot that almost never sees the sun?

When this idea crossed my mind, I felt a squeezing agony in my chest, as though the walls of the camp were closing in even further to crush its inhabitants. But I don't want to think about them now. I don't want this curse to follow me, when I am about to sit and drink a cup of coffee. I tried to expel them from my mind, but an image reinforced this comparison inside me.

When I take the subway, it is as if I am suddenly entering an underworld akin to the sort where people often take shelter from war. There is a parallel life here, and there are so many different nationalities. If you don't hurry to escape the subway, to get out at the next station, life will leave you behind. This is America; there's no room here for slow people.

You can't hide yourself in the land here, indeed you watch people coming in and going out quickly, and you know that other people are walking above this station. It's odd how civilization transforms tunnels into a way to make life easier for people. The strange thing too is that you go into a tunnel in New York and then emerge to see skyscrapers. What is the balance here between highest and lowest?

I got out of the subway and sat in a little coffee shop on the street corner. It seemed to me that I was now both here and there—at the lowest and highest point, in both Hilda's country and in New York. Wherever I am, I am a stranger. I am that stranger who someday wants compensation from the world for his alienation, who doesn't want simply to capitulate to tragedy. This is what I felt when I first came to America. Were it not for this spark, I would never have decided to forget my face and my leg and work long hours to complete my studies.

Sometimes I had somewhat plausible-seeming dreams that I was the one who had liberated Palestine. I wanted to be powerful, despite everything. Surely I would say that a lot of my toughness came from my father, the teacher who didn't succeed as a fighter.

My father was a man who wore a military uniform when he dreamed about liberating his land, and took it off when he realized that he was fighting on other people's land. He was the one who always amazed me. My mother's love for him and her regard for him as a friend, father, and invincible man made me want to be him.

If it weren't for my injured leg and the painful fear of losing Hilda, I would have sworn that I could be the ideal lover. But something about that fear was involuntary. I used to know that it controlled me, and I saw it envelop me when I refused to acknowledge it. Why, after all these years, did I admit my dreams? Where did they go? Does life discipline us like that or are victory and success an illusion? Why did I repeatedly challenge myself, as a young man, and now find myself surrendering? I don't want anything except to drown in forgetfulness. To forget even the features of my own face. What kind of punishment is this?

"I've found you a job," the employee at a research center in New York I had sent my resume told me one day when I stopped by in person. "But you have to watch out: it requires a lot of patience and concentration. You won't get any special treatment; you'll work like everyone else."

I nodded my head quickly so he would know that I agreed with what he was saying. The job was in the archive's office, and while I hadn't yet mastered English, what saved me were my Arabic language skills; for this job was all about collecting documents and information in Arabic on various topics. I used to go in every day in the early morning and work until late at night. What Phillip, the American man who hired me, taught me is that how other people see me is always based on how I see myself. Sometimes he would call me into his office and talk to me as he would with anyone else. He would begin by saying, "Sit down, sit down."

I would sit on the chair, guardedly, and he would take the papers I had prepared and look over them a bit and then take a drag of his cigarette. The way he smoked was really strange. He would take a long breath in and blow out after. Then he would wait a bit, and then do it again, as if there was a specific amount of time that should pass between each breath, as if his cigarette should be smoked at its own rhythm.

He knew Arabic very well and spoke it with me. He told me he had worked in the Middle East for a long time. He used to talk to me without me asking, and he encouraged my work. "Do you know you were a challenge at first? I figured I'd hire someone unusual and see the result. The truth is, you've surprised me. You don't act as if you need special treatment. On the contrary, you work much more diligently than other people. This is distinctive."

I thanked him, and he told me there was no need for thanks. He just said, "Keep at it." I smiled and felt proud.

Another time, we were talking about his country and my country. He always used to surprise me with his opinions: blunt and real. "We are a country built on the destruction of the natives; we won't hesitate to establish a country that will be an ally in the destruction of your land. America is this land of dreams because it is like this dream; it is deceptive and promises many things. It might be honest with you, but everything here is based on impulse and building things fast, just like it is. This speed eliminates anything in its path, like bulldozers, roughly taking everything in its way. This country doesn't like failure, it is about remaining above everything, at the top of the towers."

"But there is also the subway."

He laughed.

"The subway is almost the only real thing in this country. It is a place where you get real life."

I asked him why its citizens like America if they see its harshness. He said that power makes you blind and causes you to close your eyes to many things.

"There is a level of freedom here that you don't find anywhere else, that isn't easy to come by."

Once again, he invited me into his office and offered to help me go to university. He said it to me matter-of-factly, as if he were disregarding my hopes, not in a bad way but rather just taking them lightly. He picked up the phone and spoke to one of his friends. He informed me that he would help me to register at Columbia University.

"You can be happy and hug me if you want," he said, because he knew how happy I was. I really did hug him tightly, and he patted me on the back.

"Really?" I asked. "Columbia? It's the most famous university in Manhattan."

He said, laughing, "Yes, Manhattan the place that Peter Minuit helped us buy from the Indians for just sixty guilders. Do you know that it was the equivalent then to only about a thousand dollars today? We bought all of Manhattan for one thousand dollars, and they say that we aren't a lucky people?"

That night I rushed home, wanting to leap over the distance, to convey the good news to my father. He was so happy he started crying. He put his hands over one eye and closed the other. I went over and kissed his hand. I looked at his long neck and it seemed to me that his delicate skin was hiding sorrow. Something about his neck always struck me, as if its length or its girth could hide all the suffering it was possible for a human to bear, as if it was the distance heartbreak must travel before escaping.

There was new hope in our house. As if life had stopped being merely a way station for suffering. That night I understood my father's difficult decision for us to leave. I thought we could, perhaps after we immigrated—even though we were far away from our people in the camp—do more for Palestine.

Now, that I had made great strides toward success, I started to be afraid that the Palestinians would forget their land when they were far away. I started fearing that my own success was no longer connected to my land, which I did not know, because I hadn't managed to keep its flame burning inside of me as I should have.

When my father was alive I was more connected to the idea of the nation and the land. At that time, I didn't believe his fantasy that my mother was waiting for us there, but I now know very well that my father wasn't hallucinating. He was simply afraid we would forget. Mothers are the land. That is the mother my father was talking about. Now I started to understand. My father wasn't mentally unstable and his balance wasn't shaken by my mother's death. He was wiser and braver than that.

He was stubborn and determined. It's the same determination that shone in the eyes of the farmers who, he would tell me, tilled their land in Kafr Yasif before the occupation. He used to say that the love of our soil would stay in his heart forever, as if he were one of those farmers. Everyone who wanted to hold onto their nation needed to preserve this relationship to the land. Once I asked him why we had to have nations as our basis. Why doesn't everyone live in all places? Why do we divide lands into countries?

"To protect ourselves from each other."

"I mean, why don't we all come from the same place, Dad? Aren't all people connected in some way or another?"

"Yes, they are, but there are interests. And the survival instinct."

"Why this stupidity? Survival is only threatened by wars, tragedies, and hatred."

"I don't know, son. But I do know that we were an unarmed people whom power colluded against. They expelled us from our place. Don't ask me how Palestine became occupied. They expelled us by intimidation. They assaulted us. They never respected us. The massacres Hitler committed against them don't interest me. They can go to hell. We can't empathize with people who are murdering us and dispersing our families. You ask me what the nation is? Why don't we all live in peace and love? Because we are stupid, or because our land is squeezing us out? I don't know. It doesn't matter to me. I know that the nation is that tiny space you can call home. Imagine yourself without a home. We aren't hippies. Hippies are foolish dreamers. The nation is what helps you maintain your dignity and sovereignty. Outside your land, you are a slave. That's human nature; it understands neither tenderness nor humility. Life is ferocious; it needs a nation. Americans rushed from all corners of the globe, greedy for free lands. Land is your only space and your only freedom. They came and took everything from us."

My father was silent for a minute then continued bitterly, "Sons of bitches, they're all sons of bitches. Whoever intimidates you is a son of a bitch, and neither conscience nor conversation will benefit him."

"You ask me what a nation is. It is belonging to life. To belong, you can't agree to be oppressed, or then you only belong to your own world. Perhaps Palestine isn't the most beautiful patch of land on earth, son, but that's where our dignity is."

Our dignity. Yes. Do you know why it is our dignity, Dad? Because if we don't return, it isn't distance that will destroy us, but rather these murderous feelings of injustice. Do you know why I respect you and miss you, Dad? Because your love for your land was as pure as it is. Do you know why I can't be like you? Perhaps because I never lived there.

Perhaps it was because I never knew its beauty that I retained only a ravaged image of the land. You all are the generation who experienced displacement, who were stung by the enemy's weapons, and we are the ones who didn't know and indeed harvested what you sowed. I see them on television screens, Dad, and hear them speaking, but I don't know if that's enough to become a part of them.

You say that our dignity is there, and I say that suffering is here. I say that I can't lift myself out of these feelings that I am defeated, Dad. I don't know where you got this strength to carry your children and emigrate with them, to resist the temptation to fight.

You can deceive yourself, struggle on a land not your own, and convince yourself that the major slogans are justified, but you withdrew from the battle before it wore you down. How can we, as Palestinians, Dad, preserve our collective knowledge and distinguish right from wrong? Our accounts of things are all jumbled up and full of anger. How can a person mired in suffering know how to distinguish between what should and should not be done? Should we hold the poor accountable for stealing when it's their last resort?

You saw that our fight in Lebanon was a mistake and you left. But in moments of despair, Dad, I can only blame the whole world for our misfortune. I blame God and lose faith in him. But you aren't here anymore to answer my questions. What will happen next? Will we return some day? You left me while still clinging to your faith in our return, but you didn't leave me a road map. How can I have faith like you did, Dad? How can I believe that a woman who lived all her life thinking that we were evil people—a people who wanted to occupy her country—loves me?

How was Hilda passing her time far away, on the other side of the world? I was curious. Had she told any of her family or friends about me? Did she remember me? I now called my relatives in the camp more often, as if trying to shorten the path to her, as if I myself was ready to return, to go back to the past, to dive into the country that had hosted my family and me, even if reluctantly. I imagined her among those people who hated us Palestinians so much, who considered us the cause of the war and the destruction of their country. Would she dare stick up for me?

I used to imagine them all gathered together and ask myself what they might be talking about. What stories they might be telling. What did Hilda tell them about what she did in America, about dancing, about her show that I didn't attend?

-3-

Mount Lebanon, 2000
Hilda

"You left the country to dance? Is this sane in any way?" My father's friend asked.

"This is an important part of my dream," I answered, and then explained in more depth the science of the body and the importance of expressing an absolute state of unity with the air and music while moving to the body's melodies.

My dad didn't hear. He pretended he was listening but he wasn't convinced. He was happy that his daughter, the symbol of his open-mindedness because I lived in the West, had realized a dream of his—belonging to a superior world … or something like that. This is what made him accept the idea of me traveling abroad, to boast that his daughter was living in one of the most powerful countries in the world. He wanted to seem open-minded and perhaps hoped to follow me, to settle the whole family there.

He was warm to everything connected to the West, as if it were a perfect, flawless world, and he used to always ask me if I had fallen in love with one of Uncle

Sam's citizens. I asked him once what if I had fallen in love with an Arab man over there—say, a Syrian, Gulf Arab, or Palestinian?

He laughed hysterically, as if convinced that that was totally out of the question. He was waiting for me to love someone called George, Andrew, or Mark, and didn't expect me to say, for example, that I'd met someone called Muhammad when abroad in the West.

"You couldn't do something like that, I'm sure."

"What makes you so sure of that?"

"I know very well how you were raised—you're not that type."

"What does 'that type' mean?"

"You lived an open life here with us. The freedom we gave you won't allow you to fall in love with a strict Muslim boy who will deprive you of that."

"But am I not free, Dad?"

"The issue here goes beyond freedom. You are the fruit of everything planted in you. It will exhaust you to be in love with someone unlike you. You'll find yourself powerless."

I wanted to tell him, "Damn you and your freedom that you planted in me. It was a one-sided freedom, Dad, the freedom of the powerful that is totally different than the freedom of the powerless. Our freedom came from victory, or imagined superiority; from feudalism, from our belonging to a big and well-established family, from a family that never knew shame for what it perpetrated, a family no one dared ever to attempt to conquer or subjugate. Wherever I turned in the house there were banners and medals of victory, pictures of my grandfather and great-grandfather and great-great grandfather. Never was I told why we were so great. I was told only that my uncle killed himself because he was a hero."

"Three Palestinians approached him during the war," you told me, Dad, when I was a girl while arranging his medals one day. "He was headed to West Beirut on a military mission. He was one of the star officers in the military academy. Look at the medals he received."

"I warned him not to go," you said, "but he was stubborn. Our whole family line is stubborn. Look at you as well, you cling on to your opinions and you never go back on them. He went there and they intercepted him. Three Palestinians."

I used to repeat the number and the nationality to fix a picture in my mind. I saw three Palestinians wearing *keffiyehs* killing my uncle, and I felt that they—that race of people, as you said—were nothing but criminals and bandits.

I now know that they didn't kill him, but you told me the story as if they did. "They put him in their car at the Bechara El Khoury junction and tried to take his weapon. Do you know what it means for a military officer to be stripped of his weapon? This is a major insult. He felt ashamed. He couldn't handle the situation. He resisted, pointed his weapon at them, killed them, and came back home. He went in his room, locked the door, and killed himself with the very same gun. He couldn't bear to be a murderer. He was a real man in every sense of the word."

This was the end of your story about my uncle, except for the following scene: "Months after he died, some people showed up carrying a black bag. Inside of it was his daughter. She was wounded by shrapnel and died. She was only nine years old and beautiful. No, a really great beauty. She looked a bit like you. If she were still alive she would be almost your age, a little older. It's good that he died before her. They are together in heaven now."

"But why did they put her in a black bag?"

"That's what happened in the war. There weren't enough white shrouds to bury all the dead bodies in."

"Why didn't his wife ever come visit us?"

"She went to live in Beirut. Afterward, she married a man from the Kaadeh family, Amaal Kaadeh." I used to repeat her name with her new husband's surname many times angrily, as if she were a fallen woman who didn't respect my uncle's memory.

"But she came to my grandfather's funeral, she didn't forget us."

"She has no shame! If not for the sanctity of the dead, I would have kicked her out."

"Why?"

No answer.

So my uncle died because he couldn't handle being a murderer, but he killed because he felt humiliated. And then he killed himself because he couldn't handle killing. And who were they, those Palestinians he'd killed? How did one man defeat three men when they were the attackers and he was in their car? And his wife didn't respect our family or his memory. What is the missing piece of this puzzle?

His picture was the centerpiece of our house, and I was afraid of it when I was alone in the room, as if I were facing death, as if he would come out of the picture itself. You admitted that sometimes he was moody and aggressive and everyone was afraid of him, even you, his youngest brother. You didn't dare to stay too close to him too much when you were little, that's what you told me. But you loved him a lot, more than your father and your other siblings. He was my favorite uncle, as you know. Was he my favorite because he died, and because dead people take away with them both our bad memories of them and also our ability to criticize them in the face of the sanctity of their dying breath?

This story is one of the few tales of the war you told me. When I asked you if you had killed any of them in battle, you didn't answer. Sometimes your gaze denied it, other times you seemed as if you'd killed a huge number and were proud of what you had done. You never really answered me. You used to say that whether you killed or didn't wasn't important. "It's called war," was the only answer I could get out of you, as if this word set up the ambiguous possibility that you had killed.

Uncle George was the bravest in admitting that he had murdered. He used to say that he would stand at one of the checkpoints and slaughter them "for their identity cards." Once I asked him what it meant to slaughter for an identity card. "It means someone who isn't like us, we kill them before they kill us."

"So that's what slaughtering for an identity card is. Who were those people, "them"? Palestinians? Lebanese? Or Muslims?"

"They were killing us too. It's called war. We were strong.... Oh, how we were strong."

"But didn't they have names?"

"No, they didn't have anything. They're all the same. You want me to lie to you and perform my repentance. The truth is that I don't know if I do repent. They used to tell us to kill and we did it."

"Who told you to kill?"

"The party."

"Which party?"

"You know which party."

"That's it, simply enough."

"What do you want? Do you want to drag the act of contrition out of me? I told you I don't know how to evaluate things now. We carried weapons because everyone carried weapons. It isn't possible to remain defenseless in the jungle—you'll be devoured by wild beasts. And we were also dreaming of our great Lebanon. We wanted it to be a nation for only us. Foreigners were flocking to it, as if it were open to them. What would you do now if you saw strangers coming to live in your house? Would you open your door to them?"

"But were they searching for shelter?"

"Someone searching for shelter doesn't carry a weapon.... And why are you insisting on exhuming old records if the state itself doesn't even settle its accounts?"

"What state?"

"The government ... the powers."

"But you all are a part of this power."

"No, no, no. This isn't how things were. People feared us."

"But my dad changed, he's no longer ..."

"He's no longer what? No one changed. Time is what

changed. Our time is no more, my girl."

My uncle was frustrated. He believed that Christians were the only ones the war hurt, that others had been dominating them. Even the West no longer lent them a helping hand. It left them failing and extended its powers over Lebanon. But my father believed that his hereditary power would be restored. For him it was only a matter of time. He was making a huge political effort to restore his old authority. He went to Sunday mass and strengthened his relationship with the clergy. He exploited his youngest son to remember his struggles and his steadfastness for Greater Lebanon, a nation of institutions, the Switzerland of the Middle East. He took us on tours of the villages and showed us both the greenery stretched out in front of us and the sea, invisible behind it. "This beauty incites greed. We protected it so no one would plunder it. God will reward us in the end."

-4-

My friend Mohsen is also from the war generation. But he wasn't a fighter. Leaving was his choice. He threatened his mother that if she didn't pay the price of his ticket, he would fight and join the communist party. He stood under their house's balcony on Kaskas Street, in Beirut, with some of the fighters. He held his friend's gun and called his mother to come look at him.

She ordered him to come home right then. She told him that she would sell a piece of her jewelry to subsidize the price of the trip. "As soon as possible, if you can travel, you will travel," she said. Laid bare from the heartbreak of mothers, she loved her son more than his siblings. She couldn't tolerate the sight of him holding a weapon. She feared if he remained here he would be destroyed and so she gave in to him. The war robbed them of many relatives, and she swore she would kill herself if she saw her son among the dead.

What brought Mohsen and me together was the feeling that we were better than other people and that we were able to do what we wanted because we came from painful experiences. But he seemed different from me, as if he were fleeing and victorious in his escape:

handsome and the center of everyone's attention because he imposed his presence on them, as if out to head off rejection. One time I asked him not to be afraid of rejection by the society he lived in.

Insisting that he didn't, Mohsen pointed to a cross hanging around his neck, though he was a Muslim. He said he didn't believe in any of his forefathers' idle chatter about homelands, and that since he'd come to America he'd felt that he belonged here more than to any other place. But didn't America throw you far away, Mike? Where would you return after announcing your failure if not to your homeland? His answer to this question in absentia was inevitably that he was returning one day, returning to America.

He packed his suitcases, sold the last of the antiques he had in his house, and wound up all of his work. He wore ivory-colored cowboy boots and a white shirt, and used a hand to smooth his hair back. He didn't look like a loser. He didn't look like anyone but himself.

Women in his bed. Two women, three and four sometimes. Mike was totally absorbed in promiscuity and drunkenness. And then afterward, bouts of nostalgia, the story of his friend who died in the war, and his mother, whom he couldn't see because he was abroad.

But never did I feel that his complaining was out of pain. Rather, it seemed the result of excessive drinking and a certain desire to drive himself right to the brink. An involuntary desire. This wasn't out of nostalgia but merely selfish emotions. Even what he said about his family was linked to his experiences and achievements, not to other people.

Only once was Mohsen honest, about his breakdown—if only for a moment. He took this collapse like just a part of life, as a curiosity. Late one night Eva, the woman he really loved, came to his apartment unannounced. Mike was wrapped up with another woman in bed. He was cheating on Eva as if it were his legitimate right to do so or a normal part of the strangeness of his life.

It wasn't an aggressive betrayal, but Mohsen was used to being surrounded by many women. He was afraid of coming together, being folded into other bodies. Eva, the beautiful Mexican woman with her dark brown hair, big blue eyes, and slim build, came in. The impossible woman whose body was totally in harmony with her facial features. She was powerfully built and always elegant.

"Am I interrupting you?" She asked Mike while he was raptly entering the woman he was with in bed. He got off of her quickly and put his hand on his penis as if he were hiding it, and the traces of his betrayal along with it.

"Finish up at your leisure. I'm just here to collect a few things. No need to be distraught, Mike."

Mike's friend collected herself, pulled a white sheet over her body, and got ready to leave.

"No need for that," said Eva. "Stay here, you little slut. Your spot's still warm."

But Mike indicated she should leave and she did. She wasn't jealous; she knew he had a girlfriend and that she was only a passing fling. He asked Eva to sit down and told her that he would explain things to her, that things weren't as they seemed.

He put his hand over his mouth like someone trying to draw words out, not repel them, but she approached him ferociously, took his hand away, and put it on his penis.

"You need to just leave it there. Close your mouth and listen to what I am going to tell you now, you idiot. Do you see this ass that you used to say was yours when you were having sex with me? Do you see these bosoms?"

She said this, pointing at certain body parts.

"Do you see all this, you miserable man? How do you know that I haven't cheated on you like you've cheated on me? I can walk out of here right now and leave you with so many possibilities. I can leave and you will remember every time you bite the lips of another woman that when you were with me, I also used to bite."

"What are you saying, for God's sake? Eva, are you cheating on me?"

"No, things aren't as they seem."

"I want to know."

She was silent. He twisted her arm and screamed at her, "I want to know!"

She moved his arm away with even greater fury. "You want to know. Don't touch me, idiot. What do you think? I was listening to all those women and sitting alone crying over my lost love? Do you really think so?"

She pointed to her heart and said to him in Spanish, "*De mi corazon, de mi corazon.* In my country, my stupid man, it means heart. When my grandmother took me to church on Sunday, she would give me advice about my heart and say, 'if your heart is doing well, you are doing well.' She helped me take care of it well. She used to say many things, including the fact that things happen like that. 'Blind the person who stabs you in the eye!'"

"Lowlifes like you passed through our poor neighborhood and always tried to put their hands on my ass. I used to always kick them if they tried to get too near me. I wasn't like your little sluts. Neither your vanities nor your conquests make me jealous. I cared about you and you didn't respect that. I was with you because you were strong and stupid, and could give me what I needed."

Eva continued: "Do you think I didn't know? Their scents that would always linger on your clothes, the hand you would touch my body with, gave you away. Something was always missing. My moans, which would fill the room, were perhaps feelings of distress because I was choking on the perfume of your whores and groaning. I would groan beneath you and groan in other men's beds, because you lied to me. I loved you in the beginning and was faithful. I swear on my grandmother's life that I was faithful, but you let me down. But I couldn't break up with you and I had gotten used to your affluent lifestyle."

"Shut up!"

"Oh no, we are still at the beginning."

"Shut up!"

"I drank twice as much as I used to drink. Sometimes I would come to you straight after finishing with my lover. You know what? Once, I left a man's sperm stains on my hand and when I came over I wiped them on your face and your body."

"Shut up, bitch!"

"Bitch, say what? You're the bitch. You know? Sometimes I had sex with them here when you were away. This bed of sin is the best evidence of how filthy the two of us are. What did you want me to do? How can

I stand that you prefer other women over me? How can you explain that, lover? Do you want to know more or is that enough?

"Shut up."

"I got pregnant by you and I had an abortion without telling you. I didn't want you to be the father of my child. You don't deserve it. I had an abortion and touched the blood, smearing it on my chest as if renouncing my right to motherhood."

"Shut up."

"In passing I thought about what I would have named him if I hadn't killed him. What if she'd been a girl? I thought he might have been like you and I killed him, and I thought that if she had been a girl, then no doubt God would have sent bad men her way in revenge against her father. I killed it all—the possibility of motherhood, girls, boys. I killed Eva. I stripped her of everything she knew from the poorest neighborhoods in Mexico, except the ability to kick back."

"Why? Why?" He asked her while holding back tears.

"Cry like a widow, like a fag."

"Get out of here."

"You think you're so smart, and you have conquered everything and made a fortune here. You think you were tricking me the whole time. Look at my belly; you know that it isn't the first child I've aborted. You know that my mother's husband got me pregnant before. You know how fragile I was. Don't you know that, you idiot?"

She said these last words and then sat on the floor, crying hysterically. He sat on his bed naked, crying as well and shouting at her, "Get out, get out!"

She kept pointing at her heart and saying, "*De mi corazon*," while biting her lower lip. He was trying to get up to hit her, but would sink back into his sobbing, like a man whom catastrophe had wrestled to the ground.

Eva left after she pulled herself together and had attacked him, destroying everything in the room. She left cursing, swearing, and spitting. She left like a woman stripped of her beauty by time, like a woman whom life had made hard. She left wiping her eyes stained with black mascara mixed with tears. She wiped her nose and ran her hand through her hair. She left and never came back.

When he tried to call her to ask her if the story of the abortion was true, she swore at him and said, "You'll die and never know, scumbag."

Mohsen was like a crazy person during this whole period. Losing money or work didn't affect him like the loss of Eva did.

"She made me feel that I was less than an animal," he told me. "I wanted to know if that bitch killed my son."

Previously, Eva had told him about her life in Mexico. How she'd run away from home after her mother's husband had raped her. "She never knew her father. He left them when she was little, and then that scumbag raped her. She used to tell me that he put his dick in her mouth when she was only twelve years old. She told her mother, who didn't believe her and hit her. They all hit her except her grandmother. Whenever she told me about herself, there was always some kind of beating in the story—by her mother, her boss, her teacher at school. I really loved her. I didn't cheat on her. It was something else. I don't know how to explain."

Mike used to say that the idea of hers that he couldn't stand was that he was merely an asshole in her life, like the other assholes she had told him about. "Can you imagine how she talks about me now?"

"She wounded me to the core. She's the only woman who's ever made me feel that I'd been hit in the jaw and it's now crooked. She hit me with a knockout punch."

But this didn't stop Mike from pursuing his random womanizing. After that, he never got involved emotionally. He would hold on to a woman for one month as an outer limit and then leave. Most of his friends distanced themselves from him after he declared bankruptcy. This didn't stop him from making new friends who weren't in any better shape at all, as if he was addicted to living on the edge, like a man drawn toward his own death.

Mike's love for Eva was honest, to a certain degree, but it wasn't enough for him to rein in his craving for other women. He even used to say that he didn't enjoy sex with the other women he was sleeping with. He used to do that to feel he was desired, to live up to the aura that had become his identity. He used to talk about New York with a special passion, saying that it was the only place where he was suited to live.

"It's like me: its lights, crowds, subway, connection to the land, skyscrapers. All of this is me. It is this place that whenever your desire for it is satiated, your desire increases again. No, actually it doubles and keeps doubling until no life outside it can satisfy you.... Now they are kicking me out! Idiots! They are accusing me of forgery and contributing to destroying the global economy. I can leave and say that they are fabricating accusations against me because

I'm an Arab, but I'm afraid to do it, to not be able to come back. I will come back to America. I will die here."

Mike was charged with tax evasion, but there wasn't sufficient evidence to convict him. His trades and gambles in the stock market lost as well. Each investment became a source of disappointment and nothing more. But he used to believe that if he took a little distance while things got better, he would be able to return and rebuild from scratch.

He saw that New York was the only place big enough for him, just as previously he believed that Christians were on a higher level than his people. His father lowered his head when he passed in front of militia checkpoints and paid monthly "protection money" to the militia leader, Hassan "Abu Wael." This was the person responsible for the area, the person who ensured the safety of his family in the neighborhood, and over whose entrance there was a black banner emblazoned with the white, printed words, "Beware of the sniper." The first time the militia went to the fabric shop his father owned, they tore things up, shouting in his face, "Why aren't you paying, why? Do you want them to destroy your shop?" Hassan put his left foot through the chair facing the cash register and threw his cigarette on the ground. "Open and let's see." His father took the key out of his back pocket, trembling. Hassan laughed, and accused him of not only being stingy but also lacking patriotism, because he let money overshadow the protection of the neighborhood. He told him that he would consider this shortsighted behavior as unintentional, but the next time he wouldn't hesitate. Now he knew very well who they were, and he was sure that the simple cloth seller would be grateful for their presence here. "Choose what you want, guys, this brother likes good people like you. Don't be shy, take something for yourselves, take what you like and let's go!" His men took cloth from the shop and the father didn't dare to object. He was biting his lip, signaling to Mohsen, who had arrived at the shop, to stay silent and not come in and confront them. He saw the anger blazing in his son's eyes as Mohsen shouted to ask what was going on. "My big brother Abu Wael is like your uncle, he's not a stranger to us," his father said to him, his eyes filled with pleading looks for his son not to take any uncalculated action.

"They're Muslims like us and were merciless with their insults," Mohsen used to say, "This is not a sectarian war; believe me, all wars are alike. You don't need a Christian, Muslim, or Druze. You don't need a Japanese, Indian, American, or Palestinian. All of these labels are interchangeable. You only need the weak and the strong."

-5-

My father once told me that one of his Lebanese friends went mad after the war. "His name was Shawqi Rahmeh. A Christian. We used to call him Abu Iliya. After the war he became an Imam. Imagine, Shawqi, an Imam. During the war he used to stand on the roofs of buildings and aim his weapon at passersby. The sniper whose bullets never missed."

"Turn the body over," Shawqi told my father one time.

"It's a woman," my father replied.

"Turn it over and move away."

"She's still breathing."

"What do you want to do? Leave her before they come. Run."

My father and his friend ran far away. He didn't know who this dead woman was, nor if she was Lebanese or Palestinian, Muslim or Christian, but he used to say he would never forget her face. He used to say that he for a long time asked himself if my mother found someone to turn her body over.

"Imagine, Shawqi, an Imam. He doesn't speak to anyone except two of the comrades from the old days.

He stands in the mosque and delivers religious sermons. I don't even know why he decided to become a Muslim."

I used to find my father's tales about the war intensely strange, and would imagine Shawqi in a white Jilbab. I always used to imagine him as mentally unstable, despite the fact that another friend of my father who became disturbed after the war was different. Adel. Just Adel. My father never called him by another name. They took him to the mental hospital, and then after a while he left to become the neighborhood lunatic. As my father tells it, Adel would become a totally balanced person when he met with Shawqi, but with everyone else he was just entirely mad.

If someone came up to him to say hello, he would scream in the person's face. The neighborhood kids would run after him, sometimes pelting him with stones, and he would run with them as if he were playing. Then he stopped and rebuked them. He transformed into a lion and the roles were reversed. They would run and he would chase them.

My father stayed in touch with his Lebanese friends after we came to America, especially Adel's daughter. She turned to him when her father's state worsened, asking my father, for example, to speak with him by phone. Shawqi had been a professional sniper, but as for Adel, he had belonged to the Communist Party and started fighting at seventeen. He used to stand behind the tanks and guns and fight fiercely, without mercy. He was obsessed with the struggle, completely, courageously absorbed by it.

But during the Israeli invasion of Beirut, he saw his brother, who was only one year younger than him, being carried as a lifeless corpse, and he knew that his brother had run away from home to fight. He went to his mother and turned the house upside down. "I'm the one who's fighting, I told you to keep him home." The bereaved mother threw her son out of the house and accused him of causing his brother's death. "He went to do what you did; he followed you, I lost him, and you don't want to stop and tomorrow I am going to lose you too. Either you stay here with me or I don't want to see you anymore."

He went out searching for his brother's killer like a madman. The killer could have been anyone, and he would never know who. Isn't this what happens in wars? No one knows who either the murderers or the murdered are. It's as if names are no longer necessary. Only bodies fall. Some of our relatives spent years searching for the bodies of their loved ones, looking and not finding them. Some of them want to know the killer: from the shape of his eyes, to his build and his stature. But no one knows.

My father and his friends occupied an apartment in Ayn El Mreisseh, where they would meet to coordinate their plans. They always deployed a guard at the bottom of the building, which was otherwise completely abandoned. The other apartment they occupied, in another building, belonged to a surgeon, and it was used not only by the men but also the women, who prepared food there for the fighters. Also according to my father, the other apartment saw births—most of the neighborhood births. During the war, as he used to say, roles were all completely turned upside down. An ordinary woman could become a nurse or a midwife, and an ordinary man would become a fighter. Destruction became a part of daily life, and if you had the good luck to be able to relax a bit, you felt an unparalleled happiness. "We used to wait for it to get cold and storm sometimes to get a break from the violence. Even in the shelters there was an intimacy between people, an intimacy that is engendered only in disasters," he used to tell me.

According to my dad, the Lebanese suffered the worst remorse after the war. The Palestinians didn't suffer psychologically as much as they suffered losses, he said. "When you fight on a land not your own, you don't believe it's your battle. After atrocities and massacres, of course most of them leave scarred, but the pain of occupation remains greater than does the pain of any war. Perhaps we believe that if we were on our own land, we would not have been as stupid as the Lebanese who were killing each other. But, son, when I see division in Palestine, I'm really unable to judge our people."

My father had a theory that our power rested in our unity alone, and that life had taken us away from the truth and pointed its compass in another direction. "Perhaps this is human nature. We are human in the end and we aren't able to struggle and resist all the time. Human beings have souls, and the soul gets weary. Human beings have bodies, and bodies have specific kinds of resilience, strength, and patience. The Israelis didn't fight only with weapons but politics as well. They fought our dignity and our courage. Sons of dogs, they destroyed us."

Hilda also used to tell me about a crazy man in her village. "I used to love him. I think he also used to be fond of me. Giorgio was his name. He was crazy but sweet, wandering the fields and cutting flowers. He carried a pack of cigarettes and almost always had one in his hand. He held them in a strange way and shook his head from side to side while he was smoking. He used to say only a few words, and sometimes he would curse all alone, as if he were quarreling with someone."

"He would end his quarrels by saying, '*khalas*,' and plug his ears as if he couldn't stand the voices he could hear in his head. The people in the village said that when he was small his mother ran away with the village priest and his father was always really hard on him and took revenge on her through him."

In his adolescence, Giorgio transformed from a reclusive boy to a crazy person. His father, who strongly regretted the way he had treated his son, almost lost his mind and then died. Giorgio's mother never came back. The boy was in the habit of going to the monastery and throwing stones at it, but the monks would take pity on him. The villagers also felt sorry for him and would feed him, until finally one of the old men gave him a little room in a faraway orchard to sleep in.

Laurice used to visit crazy Giorgio there to clean the house his room was in. She said his room was haunted by an afreet. She collected bits of food off the floor and put the bedclothes outside in the sun. She dusted and opened the window to let in some sun and air, because according to her, angels won't enter a house without sunlight.

Hilda used to tell me about Laurice's visits to the crazy man when he was sick. She would rock him like a little baby and tell him, "Open your mouth, look, the birdie is flying in," and he would give a belly laugh. If it weren't for the fact that everyone in the whole village used to know his real mother and the midwife who attended his birth, they would have all thought he was Laurice's son.

But the only thing that used to vex Giorgio and make him want to attack Laurice was her request, "Recite the Our Father."

He used to rebuff her, even when she insisted, with tears in her eyes, "Please for the sake of the holy cross, recite the Our Father." He used to turn to her, open his arms as wide as he could, and scream, making the sound "Aah." If she insisted, he would heighten the tone of his screams: "Aah, aah, aah."

"He'll never recite it ever, enough trying," Hilda used to tell her.

"My heart is breaking for you, it's breaking," Laurice would lament while he would keep on with the same rhythm, "Aah, aah, aah."

Laurice was simple enough that she didn't believe that the boy nurtured hatred against the monks because one of them had run away with his mother. She believed that no one, no matter who, would dare question his faith in God's emissaries, and she used to say that his mother ran off as a result of his father having oppressed her. Indeed, she was so naïve as to say, "The priest just wanted to save her from this torture," insisting that that was the only reason he had run away with her.

Hilda asked me, "Why do *you* think he ran off with her?"

"Surely he was in love with her."

"The villagers said that she used to go to church to confess, and he would hear her confession."

"Surely he loved her a lot," I replied.

"But how could she just abandon her son?" Hilda asked.

"She loved him a lot, too."

"But do we love to this degree? What love allows a woman to destroy her son's life?"

"Perhaps that was his destiny," I reasoned.

"Perhaps if she had stayed things would have been different."

"And perhaps the father would have run away, too."

"Do you think that the blame falls only on the father?"

"He could have spared his son the consequences of the mother's sin."

"But aren't you the one who said that we sometimes lose control?"

"Yes, that was me," I admitted.

"Do you feel forgiveness toward him?"

"There's no forgiveness for crushing a child."

"Do you love me?"

"More than you imagine."

"But you don't find forgiveness justified after we reach a certain breaking point?"

"Why are you saying this now?"

"I'm thinking out loud about whether there are things that—at the end of the day—are measured by their results. Can beautiful things remain or do they merely become ugly in the end?"

"I love you."

"Would you have run away with me if you had been in the place of that priest?"

"I don't know."

"Do you think he was brave?"

"Yes."

"Was she selfish?"

"I don't know. What do you think?"

"Perhaps she is a terrible, harsh woman. Truly. I don't know what I should think. I know I pity him. I pity her, too, both of them."

"Maybe he is happy being crazy."

"No one chooses to be crazy."

"Indeed they do, dear. Many people do that."

"Society pushes them to. So it's not a choice. It is a state of mind linked to many factors."

"Why did we start talking about madness?"

"Because I'm crazy about you."

Hilda laughed out loud and came over to me, asking me to hug her. I pulled her close. Then she fell asleep and left me with only her fragrance and tales of madmen. Insomnia haunted me. Whenever I started thinking that I would never have the courage of the fugitive priest and one day I would let her slip between my fingers, I would get distressed and break out in a sweat. I went over and kissed her like someone planting seedlings in the soil, tenderly hoping they would grow.

Whenever I would approach Hilda, my lips would tremble more and more until they were fixed on her body, imprinting a kiss. I could keep kissing her when she was asleep and submissive. I also wanted to run my mouth all over her skin without waking her, and touch her after that without her looking at me.

-6-

New York, 2000

Marianne was sitting in the corner, cigarette in hand and crying. She pulled her hair back with her hand and sobbed. I sat in front of her looking only at her. She asked me if I found her pretty and I told her yes.

"You are very pretty."

"Why do you think he left me, then?"

"He didn't leave you, my friend."

"He chose to go to war. Why didn't he refuse?"

"Because it was his duty. Perhaps you won't be able to see things as he saw them, but he thought he was doing the right thing."

"If he loved me he wouldn't have gone."

"Why are you making this equation?"

"Do you love Hilda?"

"Why are you asking this question?"

"Answer me, do you love her?"

"Yes, more than you can imagine."

"Why did you let her leave, then?"

"She would have left sooner or later. And I didn't let her go. It was her choice."

"Why aren't you responding to her messages?"

"Because I don't want these messages, I want her."

"Why don't you let her know that?"

"I don't want to."

"You don't love her."

"You can't determine what I feel."

"He didn't love me enough to stay here."

"Why do you insist on punishing the man by abusing his memory? We all know well that he loved you and the children a lot. Didn't he tell his friend how much he was suffering? Didn't you tell me that he used to relieve himself outside, since there were no toilets or anything where he was fighting? Didn't you tell me that he wrote to you that he had reasons that pushed him to join up for this war? Why would he have done all of that if he didn't love you?"

"I don't know. I know that I've been hanging on to this vortex for years and I don't have an answer for my children about their father's fate. There are so many things I don't know. If I am a woman or a man; if I have lost my femininity. Do you know how many beds I have run away from? I can't see one more man inside me. I loved him; I carried his children inside my body, and we used to contemplate my belly together, waiting for the baby to come out. He would laugh when I told him that I felt my belly was like a rising and falling wave."

Marianne was silent. She lit another cigarette. She pushed her hair back again. She had stopped lamenting. She asked me if I thought he was still alive.

I didn't know how to answer. For a moment, I thought about the impossibility of the man being alive, with there being no sign of him, however minimal, but I felt that I couldn't say that to her. You can't be frank about the truth with a person steeped in depression and misery and you can't slap them in the face with it. This slap in the face will wake them from the illusions they believe in. On the contrary, you empathize with this illusion and it pulls you further in.

I couldn't give this slap, at least not then, in those circumstances.

I stayed silent. Marianne gave me pleading looks, as if asking me to believe in her illusions. I thought she was like my father in his refusal to accept my mother's death, as if it would mean the death of Palestine. I thought, *What if some stupid guy comes along one of these days to give me such a slap in the face, saying, for example, that there is no hope of ever returning?* Perhaps I used to want to hate this person even if I tacitly agreed with him about the difficulty of getting our land back. It's said that a courageous person can hear the truth, but I know that this is a totally false conclusion. Someone who receives the news of a death, or utter hopelessness, with equanimity is not a brave militant; he is secretly miserable and has simply learned the art of hiding pain.

Silence and looking around, exactly as if I were in an exam. Was I supposed to tell Marianne that her husband died, shaking her up with this hard fact even while embracing her? Tell her to wake up from her dream world, say we should bury him here together, cry until it's over, and then go out and live a new life? Or listen to what she wanted?

I broke my silence to say I didn't know, and this

simply caused her to break into tears again. I just wanted her to go, to leave. *Why is she asking me if he's alive? I'm not a god. Like her, I only want this tragedy to end.*

After Marianne calmed down, she got up off the floor and went to the washroom. I followed her, watching her wash her face with soap and water, massaging her cheeks with her fingers while closing her eyes. I offered her the guest room to spend the night in but she said that she had to get back to her children. She hugged me, kissed my cheeks, and said that I was a wonderful friend and that she would be fine.

I heard her car engine outside and felt calmer after she left. Not because I wasn't empathetic, but because I needed calm, perhaps even to be alone. I remembered how much hearing the sound of Hilda's car made me feel safe sometimes as I sat waiting for her to come back from her rehearsals. While waiting for that sound now, it occurred to me how much some women resemble death for no reason except that they are life. You leave them; life leaves you. Perhaps for this reason Hilda's trip made me suffer, because it made me a defeated man once again.

I don't know why she insisted on returning; I don't know why she insisted on opening up this world that she escaped from to put it all out there before me. Was this her way of punishing me? Was she moved by a desire for revenge?

The thought of never seeing her again really scared me. Was this why I'd been so afraid of her going away? Did my fear of confrontation overcome the fear of losing her? Was this the reason I wanted to distance myself from her now, with all my strength, not answering her calls and not speaking to her? What was she doing? Was she settling accounts with her past through me? Where had this timid girl who didn't dare look in the mirror when she was making love with me gone? Where had she gone, that girl whose head I used to lift, whom I would then ask to look at how the light coming from her eyes shone through her body when she was naked?

"Shining flesh," she once told me when touching her breasts. "When you come near my breasts, they shine." She said this and then smiled and hid her face in embarrassment. Then she grabbed my hand and said, "Put it here, move it, put it on my face, put your fingers on my eyes. Do you know how we can hold the world in our hands sometimes? This is how I feel when I'm with you. Like a body shrunken to become the size of a hand. I feel that I am completely safe from everything, as if I've been dancing. The steady body here starts moving up in the air, but in reverse."

That night she kissed me and asked me to hold her against my chest until she fell asleep. I did. I watched her close her eyes and imagined us dancing together. I see myself able to fly with her gracefully. I slept while at this highest point of the universe, peaceful and tranquil.

-7-

After she split up with Mike, Eva met a director who offered her a role in an American soap opera and she started appearing on the television to advertise it before its premier broadcast. Rumors were rife that she was sleeping with the producer of the series, a very rich woman. This quickly became accepted as true, after Eva, who was previously an unknown actress, moved to Fifth Avenue, one of the wealthiest streets in New York.

The Mexican woman moved to a better world than what Mohsen could afford, though he was rich, and she ascended to the world of stardom, as if she thus were reclaiming from him her squandered rights. As she always used to say, "Surely I deserve major compensation for my previous life. I won't ever settle for the least of anything." She would laugh, drink a lot, buy clothes she needed and didn't need—international brands like Chanel, Gucci, Bulgari, and Yves St Laurent, the newest cars, and the fanciest foods. "Look at this new watch, guess how much it cost?" she would tell Hilda. "Did you see these shoes? I feel excited, I only feel excited when I put a Cartier bracelet on my wrist."

But Eva never bought anything with her own money;

that is to say, from what she earned working. She always wanted to live off of someone else and put her money in a bank account. The most important feature of the men she talked to was their bank accounts. She didn't hide her materialism from Hilda. She told her about nearly everything. They became close friends in record time, and this was surprising given the lack of commonalities between them, at least on the surface.

I never knew what brought them together, nor why Hilda loved Eva so much, and refused to pass judgment on her. She described her as an intelligent woman in a cruel world, even speaking about her with excess motherliness and indulgence. "You don't know what happened to this woman," she used to say. "Everything she is doing now is a kind of revenge."

Mohsen put down the phone angrily as if Eva were inside the receiver and smoothed his hair back, slapping his forehead with the palm of his hand three times in a row as if searching for an answer.

"Leave her, man, what do you want from her?"

"I don't know, Majd. Every day I say I will forget it but anger is eating me up."

"You have different women in your bed every day.... Is it because she left you?"

"She killed my child.... How can I let her go so easily?"

"Are you sure?"

"I don't know. That's what's killing me. I don't know."

Mohsen turned off the television every time he saw Eva. Soon madness overtook him and he called her, but she responded by cursing him as usual.

"Hello … Eva? Listen to me … you bitch. You're living on Fifth Avenue now. Who's paying for you? Are you having sex with women now? Don't hang up on me … bitch."

I didn't know if his actions stemmed from his great love or feelings of loss. Many times when she didn't answer her cell phone, he called her home phone and stayed under her balcony all night, threatening that he wouldn't leave until she spoke to him.

That night she didn't call the police. I don't know if she took pity on him, but she went down wearing a robe wrapped around her sexy Mexican body. He was leaning his head on the steering wheel as she was standing in front of the window smoking a cigarette. She asked him what he wanted and he pleaded, "I want to know if you were actually pregnant and aborted the baby."

She didn't answer.

"Why did you do that?"

"Why did you cheat on me?"

"It wasn't cheating…. It was escaping intimacy."

"Spare me the ridiculous justifications, I beg you."

"We can fix everything, but I want to know."

"You won't ever know, and I don't want to fix anything."

"Why? Have you started having sex with women now?"

"Because I know that if I went back to you, you wouldn't stop having other women in your bed. You will for a few months, in the best-case scenario, and then you will go back to cheating again. You are addicted to cheating, my man."

"No, I won't do that."

"Do you yourself even believe what you are saying? And you want me to believe it?"

"I love you Eva, I love you for real. I suffocate at night because you're far away. Every other woman, every one, after I am finished with her I miss you more, exactly as if I have just proved to myself that there is so substitute for you."

"Are you listening to what you are saying, as you speak? Do you hear yourself?"

"I love you Eva, and I want you to come back to me. They want to destroy me now. I need you a lot."

"Who will destroy you?"

"The Americans, the government, everything is against me. I am begging you, Eva. The war, first of all, and now this! Don't leave me all alone!"

"Are you high? Do you think I still believe this nonsense? 'They insulted my father, they stole from our store, I saw destruction in the war.' By God, have you forgotten how many times you repeated those stories? Escape your role as someone who's failed, man. If you're truly in pain, heal yourself. Don't project your misfortunes onto me."

"I'll destroy them, all of them, and you will be my queen, Eva, my dear."

"Listen, I didn't come down here to listen to your whining. You ruined my self-image. Staying with you will do nothing but destroy me. You made me question myself daily. Why did you want other women? You made me see myself as ugly—even my hands and fingers that you used to like. I no longer knew if they were as good as some other woman's hands and fingers. I can't, I don't want to go through this again. I want you to get away from me forever, to forget you ever knew me, and to forget the story of the abortion. Everything. Just go."

She didn't wait to hear his response, turned her back and walked away. She left him alone, he who'd kicked dozens of women out of his bed. Mohsen had already asked himself hundreds of questions in the run-up to this encounter. He would lament how "life is punishing me" and would describe her as a woman who revives a man and shakes him out of his self-delusions; a woman who refuses to put herself totally at a man's mercy because she wants a partner and not torment; a woman who surprises a man not only by being absent but also by completely breaking off their relationship.

Eva walked with sure and steady feet back home and left Mohsen not knowing what to do. Where should he go now? It seemed as if someone had thrown him out of his house all of a sudden, though this was not at all what happened. He was like someone who at one moment loses control of the steering wheel and of life, like someone whose clothes have been stolen by bandits and has to hide his nakedness, like a woman who's learned that her husband has taken another wife.

He could have spent what was left of the night under Eva's balcony, not waiting for her but simply because he didn't know what else to do, like a heavy body that suddenly lost its weight but wouldn't fall down. When he went home and told me to come over, I was very honest with him. I didn't feel any empathy for his situation. "With your Arab mentality and all your machismo, you want to love a foreign woman, and you want her to accept this with an open mind? What's this about, man?

We aren't in that time, we aren't in that place."

He didn't like what I said. I at least wanted my friend to face the facts. Mike was what showed but Mohsen was what shaped him. And though it annoyed him, I never called him anything but his Arabic name. He hated me sometimes for this, but this was the first condition I put on our friendship, not to bargain with him like everyone else did and satisfy him. He would cut me off for periods and then get in touch with me unsolicited because he knew that he sometimes needed moments of true friendship, which no one among the herd surrounding him could provide.

He used to put his hand on his cheek and listen to me talk, as if he were bored with what I was saying. This had no effect on me. I kept talking, and he kept cutting me off to ask the same question: "Do you think she was really pregnant and cheated on me? If she did have an abortion, how would I know if the baby was really mine?"

"I don't know," I told him, "But this isn't what's most important. You have to forget about it and leave the girl to her own process."

He poured a glass of whiskey, nodding his head. "You're right, I'll forget the bitch."

He changed the subject and insisted on taking me on a tour of his place, describing the paintings hanging on the walls and a sculpture of a horse's head that had cost him a fortune. He held the glass in one hand and a cigarette in the other and started moving his body as if he wanted to convince me that in these few minutes that had passed he had truly succeeded in forgetting Eva and everything connected to her.

At times, I tried to sympathize with Mohsen against

Eva, and not excuse her for what she had done to him, especially when I saw him broken or angry. But I kept involuntarily pitying the girl. When I saw her on television I thought about the harassment she had suffered and imagined her mother's husband, who had raped her, seeing her as a shadow of this tragedy she'd lived through and that Hilda had told me about. I knew that Mohsen never fell short with her, that he used to meet all of her demands and satisfy her wild desire to get rich, drive the best cars, and buy clothes she needed and didn't need.

I knew how much he loved her and spoiled her, and how he had done no small part to transform her into this woman who wanted to have it all. He was the one who got her used to luxury and extravagance, and she in turn enjoyed her new role, as if she were in the opening scenes of a film: a woman who transformed from a victim into a domineering and overbearing lady. She was also the star he wanted to rescue from life's tragedy, but his bad habits got the better of him.

In spending so much of his desire on bringing many women into his bed, he wasn't successful in love. In the beginning, it didn't occur to her that this lover who lavished her with everything would ever cheat on her. She felt love, security, and satisfaction, but little by little she discovered this other side of him.

Eva was also surprised by this disparity between New York's high-rise towers and its underground world, that of the subway. Mohsen raised her to the highest summits and then brought her back down to the lowest. She tried to adapt to his temperament, she once told Hilda, but she couldn't.

She told Hilda that when she was alone with Mohsen and exclusively with him, she felt that she was the most important woman ever. "I would unbutton his shirt and kiss his whole body to make him feel like a total king, as if I wanted to swallow him up, keep him inside me. There, near his body—whether I was on the top or bottom, or in any position—I was like a woman floating on clouds in heaven. When I found out he was with other women, the idea that another woman would take him shattered me. I started to want to know where he was at all times. When he didn't answer my calls, I felt like a dog whose owner put her in a cage and locked it. I couldn't carry on anymore like that. I don't know if I was able to sacrifice for the highs because they came with the lows. But I did have to be liberated from this, no?" That's what Eva told Hilda.

Hilda compared Eva's feelings to a fall from on high. "You're at the top, on the ninety-ninth floor of your office, and then someone throws you off or something. How do you keep your balance afterward? This Mohsen never impressed me much. I don't like him."

Hilda figured Mohsen had acted so indifferently because he, being of the war generation, believed it was his right to do as he liked. "Perhaps I'm a little younger than him in years, but we are all children of those pointless battles. We can't let them give us illusory privileges because then we just regurgitate the sins of our forefathers. He is ridiculous, and I don't know what attracts you to him.

"You know why he loves America? Because for him it's a country of excuses.... 'I'm a child of the war. My friends died, I lost my family, and I'm mentally unstable. I deserve to cheat.' So he thinks. Stupid."

I used to laugh when Hilda talked about Mohsen in that cynical tone, for I knew that she didn't really hate him but rather was simply unimpressed by him. In one part of her personality, Hilda only believed in love as a sacred value, as pure love that nothing should ever be able to defile.

She used to compare it to dance and say when that the person unleashes his body to become one with the music, the whole process becomes more than merely movement. "I dance to express beauty, absolute freedom from everything: spite, hatred, and memory. When I am on stage, the musician and I are alone and, for a few distant moments, far away from thinking about what this intangibility will bring."

I told Hilda once that she was like a young woman dancing her way out of the shadows so no one could see her eyes but only follow her body. I told her that when I watched her practicing, I saw how she closed her eyes at many moments as if she wanted to free herself of her ties to life.

"I see you and I think: How beautiful is that woman? What world is she in now? Does she have a partner dancing with her in her imagination? Sometimes I see her lifting up off the ground and I really want to throw this cane out of my hand and hold her tight. You close your eyes to dance and I close my eyes to see you."

That night she slept in my lap with me holding her and playing with her hair. I kissed her forehead and then placed her head on the pillow and went to bed.

Now, looking at this sofa my girlfriend slept on, I felt how much her love had helped cleanse me of so much hatred. She changed my being and made me feel that all those enemies I had fought for years were no longer enemies.

Whenever I thought that one of her relatives might have been involved with killing my Palestinian family, I thought that now I was with one of those enemy girls. I felt a shiver run through my body. Why did she love me when she really shouldn't? That hardened enmity churned around within me; she made it changeable and open to question. I was no longer a hated Palestinian man: I was no longer a Palestinian or a man, or even a disabled person or anything at all. She loved only Majd. And this Majd confused me when he stood alone, apart from all those identities.

This was a challenge or a new birth that I resisted. Hilda was like a woman standing in the light and asking me to look at the sun when I was unable to move forward. It was easy for her to cross over and look ahead, and she'd incurred few losses in comparison to ours—a dispersed people, with endless loss. Perhaps the solution was to go out into the light and steal from life our right to some joy. But as a people whom life is killing every day, no one is able to ask us to stop dying.

Even if others empathize. Even if the whole world empathizes with us, no one understands how useless this is sometimes. Perhaps it was convenient for me that Hilda should remain the enemy. This wasn't to affect unchanging things, but her love—as much as it should have saved me—instead destroyed me. Perhaps this destruction was necessary to rebuild things, but did I really want to go out and live a new life?

I'd already done everything. I'd suffered. I'd lost my mother. Many things had ended for me. I didn't want to forget that. Why did Hilda have to dance and live up off the ground? Why did she stay with me? At times, all my love turned into hatred toward her, and a desire for her to be here plagued me, a desire to pull her to my body by her hair and watch her be terrified. In that situation she seemed to me like a little mouse totally under my control. I used to shove her face between my thighs and listen to her moan. Her voice alone was able to make me orgasm. She used to seem really weak and would suffer for me, for my pleasure. This was my only indication that she was mine in both her body and everything she had. Completely.

"You'll never find a woman who loves you like I do," she used to tell me, kissing the scar on my face. "I love you willingly. Do you know what that means? It means loving you has become my choice as time goes on; I don't need you, it's simply love."

When she said these things, I admit that I didn't understand most of what Hilda wanted to convey to me, but I enjoyed it. She also said that hers was a dangerous kind of love, because it wanted everything. She said she wanted to become one with me, to become me, and my refusal to share little details with her drove her mad. "This is dangerous. Love isn't satisfied with less than madness. This is dangerous and at times leads to destruction."

I never understood Hilda's insistence on going back "over there" even when she explained to me how her family and her past were a part of her life she couldn't ignore. She said she wanted to know everything about the place she had lived in for more than two decades but that remained haunted by secrets.

"I know my country, my village, and my family as they want to be known, but I want to see them from another perspective."

"Why?"

"You talk about Palestine, for example. It's like a dream to you, but you don't know it up close."

"I know enough."

"You know what you want to know, but you don't have the full picture.... You know occupation, people's displacement to faraway counties, and you try to be them. But perhaps if you had been there, many things would have been different."

"It's easy for you to talk like that because you aren't one of us."

"Do you hear what you are saying?"

"What am I saying?"

"Can you hear your own words? Perhaps I'm not 'one of us', as you say, but I am a part of you, or I should be at the very least. You insist on considering me some kind of enemy and you ask me why I feel so sad. You want me to be at the heart of your tragedy, but you want me to be an enemy to beat up on, too.

"No, not at all."

"And even more, believe me."

"I am sorry if I made you feel like that. I love you. I swear I love you."

In those moments, I really wasn't trying to hurt her, but it was difficult for me to express my feelings like she could or even to notice what needed to be said and not to be said to a female. I knew neither that this expression had burrowed deep inside of her nor that she used to feel that she loved me more, because she shared everything with me.

Hilda often seemed distant, as if there were a barrier between us I couldn't penetrate. A barrier I didn't even see, much less understand. She seemed, even in her clarity, to keep her life secrets hidden in her knapsack. It was as if she lived in another time and she were several women at once. She switched between innocence and maturity, laughter and tears, atheism and faith—drawing the sign of the cross on her forehead. Was she manipulating me?

I didn't understand this sharp contradiction in Hilda's personality, and when I asked her she told me, "It's so I don't get bored. You can learn to love all women in one woman." Then she laughed aloud. I used to try to interpret her laughter—was it really mysterious or merely playful in a childlike way?

Hilda used to stand in the opposite corner of the room when she put music on. She looked down, waiting for the music to start. She lifted one arm up, followed by the other, then joined her arms together as her buttocks started rising and falling. I used to ponder the harmony of her movements, her hair wrapped around her neck and then liberated.

It seemed as if a measured life was exploding—in joy or despair, I didn't know. That isn't what's important. She only danced, seeming solitary, self-contained, and fully aware of herself, as if nothing else mattered. I applauded when she finished, and she ran over to hug me and ask how her performance was.

"Wonderful, just wonderful."

"Will you come and watch me in the theater?"

"I'll go."

I told her I would go because I had no other choice at the time. But I kept wondering why I had to go. For her, this meant that I somehow was going to the end of the line with her, to the point of no return. "I'll see you there," she told me. "It means a lot to me." But I didn't want to be a helpless spectator. Perhaps I didn't want to go to the end of the line with her, given that I was still tense with a bloodstained memory—how could I be convinced that it was time to forget? That is what prevented me: the idea of denying a memory I lived within.

When she went back "over there," Hilda wrote to me in one of her letters that I was a "despicable bastard" because I had gone back on my promise to attend her performance. She said she was fed up, "Why don't you have an operation?" I read the question like a blow to my very core. She said that the scar on my face never bothered her, that she always leaned over to kiss my wounded leg, that she used to kiss my legs passionately, and that she didn't ask me to subject myself to treatment so I wouldn't think that she was disgusted by me.

"But you know what? I am no longer concerned with what you think. Why don't you at least try? I don't care if you tell me that I think you're disgusting, or that I don't appreciate the scale of the massacre. Because I'm not responsible for it. I don't care anymore if you feel that I'm merciless because I don't constantly mourn the tragedy of your country. There's no point in pity or empathy—you've never shown any toward me anyhow."

I read her letter and slammed the computer shut. Did she really intend to cause me this pain? I stayed up all night thinking about why I had never tried to fix my leg. There had been plenty of money, but this pain was a part of me. Where was Hilda when I was on my feet working long hours, with perseverance and determination, to build my little company? How could I disavow the very suffering that had made me who I was? Wasn't it necessary to display this wound to my customers openly, so they would realize how amazing I was?

Hilda also told me that my mother and father, if they were alive, would not have wanted me to remain disabled. "From how you speak about your father, he wanted you to recover. But you wouldn't do it to please him. You wanted to keep your parents tattooed on your body, a tattoo of pain."

She used to say that we often think of the dead, thinking about our own losses and feelings of collapse, and that no one cares about other peoples' losses, lives, or dreams, or whether they were deprived of happiness. Perhaps my thinking about my mother was linked to my own losses. It never occurred to me that this was selfish. When I thought about it, I knew that what she'd lost had been the life ahead of her, including the pleasure of seeing her husband and her children growing up.

"You are constantly mourning her, as if she died on purpose. You know? They didn't choose to leave. It was their destiny."

Hilda's insistence on confronting me, which I really didn't want, is what pushed me away from her. I was at peace with my misery and she came to disturb it. She came to tell me that she wouldn't stir up the past, but wanted to love me and find comfort together, going somewhere. But no. She had to know that things weren't over, especially for those of us who hadn't recovered their full rights and hadn't held anyone accountable for what had been done to us.

Part Three

- I -

Mount Lebanon, 2000

Hilda sat near Giorgio in his little room while Laurice cleaned it. They were laughing happily like children playing. Then they left her in the room and went out for a bit. Hilda didn't frighten him or treat him like he was crazy. They sat under an olive tree and she told him about America as if he completely understood what she was saying.

He nodded his head and looked around as if he were listening and not listening at the same time.

"Are you listening to me when I am speaking, Giorgio? Why don't you answer? Giorgio.... If I asked you to recite the Lord's Prayer for my sake, would you do it?"

He didn't answer; he just kept spinning around and around.

"Let's say it together. Our father who art in heaven ..."

"Aah ... aah ... aah."

"Why, my friend? Let's both recite it together for ourselves—not for their sake. I used to say it to myself, without anyone in New York hearing me, whenever I felt alone. Sometimes I used to also chant it.... *We take refuge in the shadow of your protection, Mother Mary....*"

Giorgio smiled.

"You like that? Let's recite it together."

"Aah ... aah."

"Stubborn!"

Laurice's voice cut them off, calling them to come back. She had cooked, and they all sat down at the table together. Giorgio banged his spoon on the table and laughed. Laurice went over to him. She took his hand and dipped his spoon into some soup and then raised it to his mouth. As soon as the soup touched his lips, he put his tongue out to taste it. Then he started eating by himself. He took the spoon from the top, holding it the right way, stirred the soup a bit, and then ladled it into his mouth, eating.

It didn't matter how much pain he carried inside or what had driven him mad. He was good looking, with an innocent beauty and a pure soul far removed from everyone else's noise. He was at peace with his primitive kind of life, living without hypocrisy, without making himself chant hymns or recite the act of contrition. The young man fled the horrors of mankind, relying on his unconscious and liberated from all chains, including his mind.

Hilda sat with him in the garden after eating. She was also taken by the yellow wazzal flowers that had just appeared, wanting to become one with them. She thought about Majd and talked about him with her friend, who didn't understand what she was saying.

She told Giorgio that he had chosen nothingness—freedom from the weight of the past, present, and future. It was a beautiful thing that she herself couldn't do because she wanted to immerse herself in everything and learn from it. But she was sitting in nature and thinking about all of this illogical guilt and pain her boyfriend left her prey to. She thought that flower petals don't close back up but wilt, fall, and die. Time doesn't go backward. The young woman she was before leaving this place years ago would never return. Perhaps when she went back to New York, she wouldn't be the woman Majd knew. She wrote to him, "I don't know why you chose to punish me for my love for you, nor why you aren't answering my calls. This has hurt me for days now and I've thought a long time what I've done to deserve this kind of treatment from you. I haven't discovered the answer and today I don't want to know anymore. Perhaps some things aren't meant to be interpreted. Perhaps you aren't so different from the people you labeled your 'executioners' during the war. You're like them, waiting for a scourge to ruin our love. Damn you, damn them, and damn everything else too."

Often Hilda's letters only made Majd feel resentful toward her. He looked at her angry words impotently. This resentment was stronger than him and he couldn't explain it. He resisted the happiness that was there for him to take, even though he loved her. It was here before and he enjoyed it, like having a kitten in his house.

He could still hear Hilda's loud laughter now, the laughter she would let ring out everywhere. He wasn't punishing her for anything. In reality, he didn't know what he was doing. He was afraid of the material possessions she'd left behind at his place. Sometimes he thought he should burn them all, while at other times he missed Hilda's embrace.

-2-

New York, 2000

I went out to eat dinner at a little dive on Harlem Avenue, where we lived when we first arrived in New York—a place that always used to comfort me when I started studying at Columbia University. I waited for my food, thinking about the words, "You can live here for a thousand years and you'll still be an angry Arab." Drinking a beer, I thought about the fact that I was here in America, living with hundreds of thousands of people who didn't care about my cause, and that perhaps I was even participating in justifying the existence of a Zionist entity somewhere.

Of course I'd still be an angry Arab; I didn't have the same rights as they did. This anger was my only motivation to live. I tried hard to forget it, to acclimatize myself, to become a part of this enchanting city. But like a woman whose dress pulls her back whenever she leaves her boyfriend, my fundamental being dominated me and I was not ashamed of it.

The waiter brought me the pizza I'd ordered, with lots of pepperoni. I ate quickly, like everything that happens in New York. Across from me there was a guy full of tattoos who had a strange hairdo: half of his head completely shaved, the other half parted to the side. Rarely did anyone in public places look at the scar on my face. I didn't know if this pleased or irritated me.

You see all kinds of strange sorts and types of people here, so much so that some people might think a scar is a kind of fashion. At times, my self-image seemed absurd amid all these people. Indeed, no one here would be concerned about my suffering and pain. And yet I continued to hold on to my trauma and remain a stranger among them all the same. I established few friendships with non-Arabs, and even those people had something Arablike about them. Something made my homeland my unavoidable destiny. It was the connection that I shared with the very first human being, which tied me to the very formation of humankind

Harlem Avenue, for me, was totally different than the rest of New York. The reality is that every street in this city has a particular reputation. When we arrived in the City of Lights in the middle of the 1980s, this was the only place my father could afford. Compared with the other parts of the city, to me Harlem seemed like camps for the displaced in the place we'd just left back then, the American version of Sabra and Shatila, albeit a bit more civilized. This was a street of Black Americans, and I used to laugh thinking that they were New York's Palestinians—the people who perhaps should have been able to be in the American South but had found a spot in the North and made it a home for their tumultuous lives, lives that usually ended up at the bottom of things.

We lived there because we didn't have enough money to live anywhere else and perhaps because the people there were more like us Arabs. But my father always sought to keep me far away from the drugs that were everywhere, and he used to say that we were living here only temporarily, until we found another place. He hadn't wanted to remove me from a war only for me to get caught up in another kind of war on the streets. This is why he was keen on me finishing my studies and made me work in his flower shop. The place was owned by an old man who didn't want to work anymore but also didn't want to leave the place to a young guy who'd steal from him. So my father had the perfect credentials. He moved between many jobs in his life, and I laugh now when I think about it, because they're so different from each other—teacher, fighter, flower salesman.

He used to tie a work apron around his waist and start trimming and dethorning roses. He looked thin and happy, as if freshly liberated from the heavy weapon he could no now longer carry He used to read books about different kinds of plants, flower arrangements, and the life span of every type of rose. My father was successful in this profession. He became known in the neighborhood as "Arabo." He was no longer "the Professor," but his basic English helped him a lot. "Good morning Arabo." "Good morning," he would reply in English, greeting his neighbors warmly, lifting his hand, and finishing sometimes with, "The sun is shining today." Often his new expressions would come from some film we'd seen the night before, expressions he had memorized and wanted to master by repeating.

He fit into the neighborhood smoothly and easily, but at home he remained Palestinian. He wasn't Arabo to me—my father would always be "the Professor." All of his other nicknames and uniforms seemed fake to me. He was the teacher at the UNRWA school whose wife was so proud of him. Perhaps I wanted to preserve this image of him because it was tied to the happiest period of our lives. Despite our displacement, we were a happy little family at the time. Though overcrowded, the camp was a place for all of us. If one of the women was cooking mulukhiya, its scent would waft through every house in Sabra and Shatila because every family would get a share.

I used to move in and out of all the houses freely as if we were one big family. The women would sit and talk together, and when I was a little child my mother would take me with her to meetings or women would come and meet at our house. The men would do the same, sitting on Arab-style cushions on the floor, and I accompanied my father to these sessions after I turned ten. All of them, women and men, seemed strangely familiar.

They gathered together their accents, stories, and some old things that they brought with them from Palestine. I even remember the story of the man who left the camp to work in South Lebanon for two months, and when he came back discovered that his wife had thrown away things he had brought from Palestine during our displacement. If the neighborhood elders hadn't intervened, he would have divorced her. Perhaps what saved her is that she kept a lamp they had brought from their house in the homeland.

"The lamp is still there, I didn't throw it out," she

announced as he stood at the door to the house by a small crowd of men and women who were trying to calm him down. "If it weren't for that lamp, I would have thrown you out! Go to your room." She went in, amid the trilling of the women, who were happy because he'd gone back on his decision, and it was like she was getting married again.

-3-

I met Hilda after she had been in New York for about a year. She had an internship in a fashion design office in the same building I worked in. I used to see her nearly every day. Her long hair reached about half way down her back. Her body was lithe and slender, but its thinness wasn't revolting—it was enticing. She looked so European that at first it didn't occur to me that she might be an Arab.

I heard her talking on the phone at the entrance to the building and she was speaking Arabic. This prompted me to approach her and ask her where she came from.

"I'm Lebanese. Where are you from?"

"I'm Palestinian. Palestinian, but I lived in Lebanon for a while."

"For how long?"

"Years.... Long years."

"I'm Hilda, nice to meet you," she said, holding her hand out to shake mine. I did the same. She smiled. "What's your name? You didn't tell me your name."

"Yes, of course. I'm sorry. Majd. My name's Majd."

I wasn't used to the warmth with which she spoke, nor did I know why she spoke like that. It encouraged me to invite her for a coffee. She looked at her watch and said that she finished work in about two hours and then could meet me if I was still free.

"Great. Let's meet here in two hours."

I took Hilda to a café near my office. We ate together. We stayed there talking for almost two hours. I watched her mouth move while she was eating. She chewed on only one side, and her jaw seemed to move slowly. She kept putting her hand over her mouth to stop eating and be able to talk.

"Do you know that this is the first time I am sitting with a Palestinian?"

"Really? Why?"

"We are Phalangists.... Not me, that is, but my family."

I didn't know what to reply. I was silent for a moment.

"Me too. This is the first time I am sitting with someone from the Phalangist Party."

"Not me—my family."

"Are they here with you?"

"No, they're in Lebanon."

"And what are you doing in New York alone?"

"I dance."

"You dance?"

"Yes, my specialization is in dance and fashion design. Two majors. The first is for me and the second is to make a living. I've danced since I was little and I want to become a professional."

"Become a professional?"

"Yes, to dance on the stage in shows. Dancing isn't bad. Don't worry."

"No, I don't think it's bad."

"Where are you from in Palestine?"

"Have you been to Palestine?"

"No, but what's the name of your village?"

"My father's village is Kafr Yasif and my mother is from a village called Abu Sinan. We are from the Galilee."

Hilda laughed and then apologized.

Sorry, but it's a funny name.... Abu Sinan. Why did they name it that?"

"I really don't know."

I used to try to choose my words carefully when talking to her, especially after I learned that her family belonged to the Phalangist Party. Perhaps if I had known that beforehand, I wouldn't have invited her to the café. But what happened, happened. I couldn't not be attracted to her spontaneity and way of talking. Her indifference. Not an annoying indifference, but the kind you feel shatters any affectation or expectations. I found myself talking while scrutinizing her, as if I were watching her reaction when I said something only to find her always a bit distant from what I was saying. Two expressions—either laughter or listening at her own pace and cutting me off to ask me about details: where I lived, the kind of work I did, how long I'd lived here.

"Talk Palestinian to me."

"Why?"

"I want to know how you all talk."

"What should I say?"

"Anything."

"Well, my sister, we talk like you all. It's been a long time since I have spoken Palestinian Arabic. You've taken me to an ancient place. What if I tell you, 'Speak Phalange'? We speak Arabic same as you do."

In the beginning, Hilda was like a challenge. A woman coming from far away who carried a part of my memories, especially the part that I don't know. If I had met her years before, I would have turned the table upside down when I heard who her family was. But time changes us. Emerging from a cramped cocoon out into life—mixing with different people in many countries, most of them likely to be enemies—makes you more accepting of the Other. I used to want to discover her: who she was, what she was doing here, why she agreed to sit down with me, what aroused her interest?

"Can I ask … why your face is like that?"

"I was wounded in the war."

"You didn't get plastic surgery?"

"No…."

"Your leg is also from the war?"

"Yes."

"Does talking about it bother you?"

"I don't like talking about it."

"As you like."

Our meet-ups progressed after that. I always tried to pique her interest, to have the answers to all her questions. She was intensely interested in Palestine, my past, my mother, my father, and the massacre. And, among other things about her own family, she said this: "My uncle killed three Palestinians in the war … then he killed himself. They insulted him, but I don't know what they did. That's all I know."

"He killed them?"

"Yes, they died."

"Why are you telling me about this?"

"So you know. It's the truth."

"What did they do to him for him to kill them?"

"I don't know. He was proud of himself.... They insulted him. He killed them, then killed himself when he went home because he couldn't stand the thought that he was a murderer."

She said that this was what created an ugly image of Palestinians in her memory, that they were nothing but thugs. She knew neither about the occupation of our country nor about the tragedy that we had lived through and were still living through. All she knew was that we had attacked her uncle and he had then committed suicide.

Hilda also told me that she had decided to leave her homeland because she was burdened by her family's image and expectations of her. "My father is a good man, but he doesn't see me as anything other than his little girl who should now act like a woman, like a princess, like some king's daughter. I never was able to have the kinds of conversations that fathers and daughters have. He showered me with money. He spoiled me. He bought me everything I needed and even things I didn't need. Imagine, even now he still sends me an allowance. All the expenses for my lessons ... everything. He won't allow me to spend money on myself, only he can.

I didn't understand how such a situation could be annoying. Lots of girls could only dream of having a father like Hilda's. But as she saw it, this was her father's means of keeping her under his wing and within the confines of the family. She used to tell me that this intense familial love transforms into a burden, preventing you from being you. She wanted to discover herself far away from everything.

"Believe me, there are people who live their whole lives without knowing who they are, what they want, and if they're happy. I have taken the ultimate step. My path isn't easy, I assure you, but it is my path."

Hilda told me that what worried her most was that she always questioned if she had made the right decisions, and most of the time she seemed harsher with herself than I suspect she really was.

"When you go against your roots, it can shake up your entire being, exactly like a plant. Imagine that a certain plant wanted to visit another bit of land, to know a different side of the sun. It might die. I don't know what would happen. I am that plant who felt that the feet of people walking by would tread on it, so I uprooted myself and left."

She also said that she liked the place she came from though it made her suffer a lot. "Perhaps if I had loved it more it wouldn't hurt me, exactly like Palestine hurts you. Perhaps Palestine is different because it didn't harm you on purpose. You didn't test it to see if it would welcome you in, as you have to in countries that don't welcome their own people. You don't see it oppressing its people and subjecting them to war and tragedy on purpose. You know it as occupied and oppressed."

But Palestine makes me feel weak, my dear, exactly as if there were some kind of hammer knocking me lower and lower down, as if my mother really were there and I wasn't able to reach her. Perhaps the tragedy of war destroys the idea of the homeland, but occupation feeds our love for it. Injustice unifies us and brings us together with our land, where this coming together and painful love is difficult to traverse. That's because these things are found inside of us and not on the actual land itself, especially for those of us who are displaced migrants, far from our land. Perhaps that's different for people who live inside their homeland. Perhaps they want to escape sometimes but the person who's run away remains just that. The idea of running away itself reminds you of what you've fled and this can be a curse.

This was my reply to Hilda. I felt that she was on the verge of tears that day. She was coming closer to me, as if searching for something. She wanted me to take her in my arms. She lifted her hand and stuck her palm on her forehead.

"I too am running away and I need to go back so I know."

"But you do know. Isn't that's why you ran away?"

"I know that I need to go back there and see them—to hear them out and talk to them. I wish you could understand that. Sometimes I'm scared, like that uprooted plant who misses the soil it was planted in, its land."

"Am I not your land, Hilda?"

"You're more than that and you know I love you a lot. But this is something different."

"Why?"

"You'll get angry if I tell you."

"No, I won't get angry."

"You say you won't get angry, but you will."

"Tell me."

"You want me to be how you picture me. You don't want to share the most important thing in my life. You don't want to see me dancing. You don't want me to get to know my past. You taught me to look at myself in bed when I am naked. Now that I have become brave enough, you don't want to look at me yourself. You think it's easy for me not to feel alienated and homesick. I believe that both of these things are a legacy we can't escape from, even if we want to. Perhaps it's human nature to constantly remember our early childhood. I don't know what will happen when I go back or if the place will cause me to suffer a lot but I know that it is necessary for me to go."

"Why are you talking to me like this?"

"Because you asked me and because I am telling you how I feel."

"Am I wrong to want you here close to me?"

"No, but you don't see what's inside me."

"Go, Hilda, if that's your decision."

I told her "Go!" and I took my distance. I didn't pull her into my arms and I didn't finish the conversation. I didn't want to understand. I didn't want to hug her, either. Why do that if my embrace wasn't enough of a homeland? Didn't she make all of these life decisions? I wanted her to go to her family, to go to her past, if only so she'd come back to me weak and submissive. Then I would decide if I wanted to hug her.

Nothing bothers a man more than the idea that his woman would find him inadequate, regardless of whether he really did satisfy her. I wanted to become everything to her. At the beginning, when we would see each other I would avoid standing right in front of her, I'd be early for our dates, so I could sit down before she got there and she wouldn't be reminded that I was disabled.

When I used to stand up at the end of a date, I would make a huge effort to appear balanced and firm on my feet. Of course I would refuse any offer she'd make to help me get up or to lean against her. I would shoot her sharp looks until she stopped offering. When I started being intimate with her I tried to control every scenario. I would tell her to stand or sit or lie down in a certain way. I would ask her to close her eyes or open them. To avoid appearing unable to control our sex life, I wouldn't let my physical problems hinder my passion for her.

Sometimes, after we finished making love, Hilda would kiss my chest and then fall asleep with her head resting there. Other times she would kiss my legs. She used to say that she couldn't imagine any man but me inside of her because I was imprinted within her, as if her body was engraved in the shape of my body: the breadth of my shoulders, my height, the size of my hands, everything.

"When a man comes inside a woman, it's different from what you feel. He is inside her body. When he pulls out it seems like he's closing the door violently behind him. This is why I want us to stay like this when we finish. It seems like a small thing, but you satisfy me when you sleep with me. Not just with an orgasm—that's something ordinary we can have with anyone if we want. This is being truly satisfied."

-4-

Throughout my lifetime I learned to insist on my injury with an obstinacy of the sort that at times can become a trap, since you become a prisoner in yourself. I always wanted to be the very image of an iron man, hindered by nothing, whom life hasn't made suffer. I used to see New York as a safe haven, a city of strangers who don't know anything about me. The streets of the city were enchanting and so crowded you could become someone else. Life moved fast, blending up a fantastic mix of everything, as if it were, very simply, life.

I could go to Central Park and see people who sat for a long time just watching what was happening or other people putting mattresses on the ground, looking for a new place to sell clothes, or people going to a fast-food restaurant and then a museum. Here you see people of all backgrounds—Chinese, French, African, Indian, Mexican, and Arab—walking around together without feeling like strangers.

For a long time I used to think about what would happen if people of all these backgrounds had gone to Sabra and Shatila. The people from the camp would come out to see who was there, thinking they must be representatives of UNRWA, some other international organization, or even Israelis.

In the camp, all faces were familiar. Everyone knew each other—from the guy who sold vegetables to the one responsible for the people's committee. We even knew the Lebanese people who came by. We were isolated from the world outside, crammed until further notice into designated, cramped spaces that started as little tents and became illegal half-built structures. In a certain corner, Abu Hassan built a room without a permit so his son could get married and live there; in another, Abu Muhammad expanded his house so his growing children could have more space.

Granted, it is stupid to compare a refugee camp to New York, but why do we, people forced to leave our land, live as if we have to stay in a corner? Why do we always live on the outskirts of already established neighborhoods? Why are we deemed to be a danger or a threat to others? Most people walk in the City of Lights alongside each other and we remain an overflow to be scattered among housing units that were supposed to be only temporary.

Within every refugee camp, the hope of return is dwindling because when people have gotten used to life in a certain place—even if it's overcrowded and uncomfortable—it becomes difficult for them to leave. My father told me that when he built his first small room in Lebanon so he could get married he felt as if he was losing his ties to his suffering country.

"It's a kind of surrender engendered by the absence of choice. Little by little, because we weren't able to bear the difficult living conditions, we started wanting to feel some kind of stability. What I did, son, was to keep a map of Palestine in the house. I want you to promise to take this map with you wherever you go."

I did keep the map. I hung it on a wall at home. I could have taken it to my office but I knew that its place was in my home. My apartment was warmer. But, often, when I would look at where I lived now, at the luxury I enjoyed, I used to wonder if returning really tempted me: Did I still have the passion for the struggle that I would have, had I still been living in the center of the crisis? This substitute location was so saturated with life, with experiences, and thus so alluring, that sometimes it led me to want to forget my homeland. If I hadn't kept this scar on my face, perhaps I would have forgotten the many injustices perpetrated on my land every day. Had I not walked with a limp, I would have forgotten that there was an enemy stalking other Palestinians, torturing them, imprisoning them, and forcing them to work under its command, submitting to its tyranny every day.

No doubt I kept on in this suffering not out of masochism but instead to preserve the flames of anger—those flames that alone seemed to ensure that our rights could not simply be blown to the wind.

Just as I remember my father after his death four years ago, I remember Philip, my first boss, and how he used to tell me, "Hold on to your right to life but don't let it destroy you. No one has all of his or her rights at any given moment. Some day you will have to accept a settlement. I don't know if the solution is two states. I don't know a thing, but for sure you will have to have a settlement."

He tried to persuade me to undergo medical treatment: plastic surgery on my face and a procedure to fix my leg. Perhaps my father also would have wanted me to heal the war's effects on my body, but no one understood what I needed within myself, because I was still connected to the past. I could stay tied to memories without having to invite in the suffering that pained me every night. I used to know that life was ugly and not beautiful at all. I knew that making myself more attractive would feel to me like extracting the evil part of a story.

For me this was like a long, extended mourning period, not out of a desire to be draped in black but because death doesn't end, because the people who murder us don't apologize. This is what Hilda didn't understand. I didn't live in darkness willingly, but no one turned on the lights after all this bloodshed.

Perhaps she returned to Lebanon for the same reason, to understand and to question, so as not to run away from the past. I don't know why this settling of accounts seemed legitimate for me to undertake, but I didn't want her to do it. I wanted her to be convinced that she would be reborn with me. I didn't understand her when she said that she didn't want me to be her home and homeland, that she wanted to go back because Lebanon was a part of her and she had to see it. She had to critically examine it.

She said that she wasn't a prisoner of pain, that before she knew me she had been able to free herself of the impact of war or murder, though she hadn't been able to forget. "Forgetfulness is incapacitating, because the more you accumulate it as years pass, the more it remains inside you and takes on other forms—if you don't look for another way to understand all those memories. With it you merely become an extension of what came before you. I don't want that for myself. I want to go back and I want to find another way of thinking or at least try to find one."

I didn't understand Hilda when she was here, in New York, and I still didn't want to understand her once she left, because I was afraid of the distance between us. I was afraid of the fields she played in, the food she liked over there, the scent of her room, her mother's and father's hugs. I was afraid that she would feel at home with them and forget me. I was afraid that she would dance in front of them, that she would dance in front of someone, and the spectators would think that her body was exposed and easy to possess. I was afraid. I knew that she was not underage or silly, but I couldn't help but be afraid. I couldn't separate this love from the accompanying fears. I couldn't admit my apprehension and let it go.

What ate away at me now was a mix of anger and regret, as if this woman had become a curse trailing me, a curse comprising everything that had happened between us that I hadn't told her. I saw her jump while shaking her hair and laughing. I saw her lifting her arms up in sync with her legs that advanced two steps ahead, and then two steps behind. Her waist raced against her legs and bent gently before her body leapt up. I saw her fire and her passion, wishing I could seize them from her, even if it meant burning my hands.

Nothing is tougher on a man than crowding the woman he loves to the point of her feeling suffocated, especially when she is filled with their memories together.

I was now trying to do this every day, to hang our gallows rope and feel it slipping from around her neck to wrap around all of me, to become a cover I slipped under and cried under with no one to see.

This is what bothered me for many years, in the same way that my feelings that I couldn't protect my mother had bothered me. I used to see bullets penetrating her body, without really having seen her death and without knowing where she had been wounded or if she had suffered.

Was she in pain before she died or did she die as soon as the soldiers opened fire on her? Did they kick her belly? Who closed her eyes? Or did her eyes remain open, staring out? Did her murderer take pity on her or did he not care? Did anyone insult her? Curse her? Rape her? Why didn't my father say anything about the crime? Why didn't he blame me for her death? Why wasn't he angry with me when my injury is what made him leave her alone? Why did he never mention my sin? This surplus generosity from him was painful to me. How could I get rid of this wound, which is what brought me all this love from my father? Why couldn't Hilda understand this?

Some people are troubled that their relatives oppress them. I am troubled by my father's love. I inherited this generosity as a loan I can never repay. I used to try to preserve it by proving to him that his son deserved all this love and sacrifice. But what would he say if he were to know that I was in love with the enemy's daughter? Would he accept her among us?

-5-

My father died in the winter of 1994. He died an ordinary death. He was sick for a few months and then passed on. I had plenty of time to talk to him and bid him farewell. I hadn't yet met Hilda, and now I find myself wondering what he would have said about her. I also used to imagine what would have been said had I gone to her father's house, met him, and spoken to him.

"You murdered my family—can you imagine how painful that is?"

"You wanted to control my land. Were we supposed to just sit back and watch?"

"My mother was pregnant."

"And what do you now want from my daughter?"

"I love her.... Do you want me to describe what my mother was like?"

"My brother died because of you all."

"How do you see me right now?"

"I don't want to see you."

"You don't want to know what I think about you?"

"I don't care."

This was an imaginary conversation with an old enemy. I don't even know how it was possible to imagine this conversation. Whenever I tried to look at the past, I felt that a dark hand was picking me up and boring more holes in my body. But something was different when I spoke to Hilda. She listened to me and reassured me that I wasn't to blame, neither for my disability nor because I came from an occupied country. She used to say that oppression made us feel that we were the ones who had done something wrong.

I used to see this old enemy adamant in his refusal to admit his guilt, so we had to carry the guilt ourselves. Who had allowed Ariel Sharon to go into Sabra and Shatila? That was a big scandal. He was seen there, my father said, adding that the Israelis had taken advantage of the Christians.

"The massacre exposed everyone," my father said. "They started exchanging accusations … information … pictures.… The whole world criticized what happened and everyone started blaming each other. The Phalangists and the Israelis." My father also said that all the world's nations were liars and hypocrites. He thought they should all go to hell, because no one prevented subsequent crimes against the rights of the Palestinians. When the corpses are in the ground, everyone is in solidarity with you, because they feel sensitive about saving their own necks, as if death directly concerns them. They panic that it will reach them. Then, after a while, when the blood has dried, the dead bodies are forgotten as if they had never been there. The bodies are gathered together to give the massacre a name, as if documentation is all that collective death merits.

My father died feeling this heartbreak. I used to know from his coldness and lack of enthusiasm for life that it wasn't despair but a kind of surrender. He used to say, "We all fled to peace after the war proved not to be meaningful." It was like the stories of repentant prostitutes who lose their beauty and choose the path of God and penitence. They don't admit that sex work gave them what they had and this is why they spent their lives doing it. They moved from the tragedy that pushed them onto this road in the first place toward justifications and then to repentance. They didn't admit the charms or benefits of this profession. Evil is also temptation, just like hatred has an inexplicable charm. We humans pass the ages in glorifying good and refusing to embody it. We don't talk about the oppression that eats away at our souls and our uncertainties changing us and sometimes making us thirsty for darkness. We don't let our souls become public; they remain two souls that never meet.

I didn't want to admit to Hilda how benighted my desire was at times. I wasn't strong enough to tell her that sometimes we love so hard because we fear losing our selves. In love, as in death, letting go of your soul can be a hardship. I used to want her to bow down before me as if it were nothing less than an act of worship. I didn't want to do that to hurt her but rather to prove to her that I was a safe haven.

I wanted to draw out of her eyes the look that my mother gave my father, the look of natural women, innocent women. "Virgin land no creature has ever touched before," my father had described my mother, and that is what I wanted Hilda to be.

Was I running away from watching her dance only because of my leg, or also running from the image of a woman who wasn't virginal? Despite living here, was I of two minds? Did I want a woman like the women in the camp, who trembled if their husbands threatened to leave or divorce them? Who rush to cover their heads if strangers catch a glimpse of them?

It was hard to discover after years that I was like other expatriates who come to a new land, bringing our old selves with us. We pretend that we aren't like we were before. My struggle with Hilda wasn't linked only to my body but to her clarity. Therefore she had to reassure me all the time that she would remain my virgin land. What nonsense! All I was doing now was punishing her with my own fear! But was there any chance of going backward? Perhaps such a possibility did exist, but I wasn't strong enough to do it.

Hilda didn't know how afraid I used to be. She didn't know how many times I'd drowned in old details. I'd become a man who'd made good, but I kept carrying around the same old suffering. My clothes changed, but the feelings of anger and humiliation remained. I remember how my father carried me to Gaza Hospital when I was wounded. I remember every detail of the place. How I regained my consciousness wearing the mask the nurse had put on me. How one day I looked in the mirror for the first time after that and saw the bandages on my face. I tried to remove them, but my father drew my hand away. I was looking at my leg as if it also were strange to me. If you lose your mother, your self-esteem, your life, your brother-to-be, and your image of your father as a hero, you are apt to think that life has delivered you a blow that will be with you and not forgotten. An undeserved pain that imprints itself on your body. You can't do anything about it. It's as if suddenly you were nobody.

"I want to see my face, Dad."

"You will when the time is right."

"What happened to me?"

"Calm down, son."

I tried to feel my features under the bandages. I wanted to know if there was just total emptiness. I held back my tears until night fell and I cried alone in bed. When we went to the Haifa Hospital in Burj al-Barajneh camp, near my Auntie Zahra's house, to clean the wound a few days later, there were no mirrors. I put my hand on my cheek and saw blood flowing out. I felt the extent of the wound. The space between its beginning and end. When would I see myself?

After my face had healed a little, I saw it for the first time. I wanted to break the mirror. I started avoiding mirrors wherever I went. A lot of time passed before I was able to look at myself. With time, the feeling that I was this scar grew within me. It summed me up. I became it.

If I succeeded in escaping mirrors at the beginning, there was no escaping my foot. My auntie constantly saying, "Oh my poor boy," echoed in my ears and I tried to move quickly when walking in front of her, as if to say that I was fine and didn't need her pity. "Slowly, sweetie," she would say anxiously, and I would flare with anger, "I'm fine, I tell you I'm fine."

"Leave the boy and stop talking, you never stop talking!" my father shouted at my aunt, who went into her room pacing up and down, saying, "What did I say? I didn't say anything wrong." "Enough sister," my father said. "We're going to leave." That day she sat sobbing and complaining to God. My father took my hand and left. "It's OK son, she loves you."

Walking was truly difficult but I tried convincing my father I was doing well. When we would arrive home, I'd look at my leg while stretching it out on the bed, as if it were the cause of all my problems. I didn't play with the boys in the camp anymore. I secluded myself in my room far away from everyone most of the time. Everyone looked at me with either contempt or pity. I remember when they used to steal an hour to play football in the camp's alleyways. One day the situation was unusually calm. I went over to them and tried to kick it with my good leg. That day I fell on the ground. They all laughed. My cousin Muhammad came and helped me to get home.

"What happened?" my father asked, "Why are your clothes dirty?" I didn't answer. "He's fine, uncle," Muhammad told him. "Everything is fine." I was bedridden for days.

"May God forgive you, my son, may God forgive you."

-6-

New York, Winter 2000

Hilda spent more than six months away. She'd stopped writing and calling for more than three months and I didn't try to contact her. It seemed to me that she wasn't coming back and that I should forget her forever. Life had become routine, with no more hope of love. I was sure she had forgotten me and was happy there, and that if she wanted to come back it would be simply to collect her things. I didn't know if she would even choose to live in New York or if her passion for dance would bring her back.

At moments I was convinced that she would come back but not for me. She would come back to dance. No doubt her passion would bring her back. Or might she surrender to the land and choose to stay there? This puzzle didn't let me sleep. It was a kind of mania. How would this woman act? What was she doing there? What was she eating? Did she pick mandarin oranges off the trees, peel and eat them, and then smell them and complain about how annoyed she was because the tart residue stuck to her hands like when she was a child? Would she eat green almonds dipped in salt?

Did she go back to walking on the stone walls like she used to do when she was little? "They weren't high … but I didn't know how to walk on ordinary land like all the children in the village," she once told me.

She always used to walk along the side of the road on the dirt where there was no sidewalk. "My father used to criticize me for doing that and so did my mother: 'Hilda, you'll get your shoes dirty.' 'Hilda, will you ever keep your clothes clean.' 'Hilda …'"

She didn't listen to this advice and kept walking on the walls, even when she reached adolescence and her body started to change. Her nipples would change shape and had their own topography, as she used to describe it. "When I walked on the walls when I was a teenager, most of the village boys would follow me as if I were the geography lesson they had to discover."

"Look at her body, thin as a bamboo pole," the village women used to whisper when talking about her. "If you put a ring around it, it would slide right down to the bottom."

Hilda was lucky, because her father let her study ballet when she was young and sent her with a driver to a dance school in Jounieh twice a week. He did this because he thought it lent them an air of prestige and aristocracy. She used to study piano for the same reason. But she never found herself musically talented.

She used to say that the sounds that provoked her senses were those her body made, playing with the air. She told me that primitive humans used to take advantage of the body's rhythms because they were the most important ways of using sound at that time. "There were no ways to make sounds at the time—no piano or anything else—only clapping while dancing or the sound of the body bumping into the ground or against another body. Your feet stamping on the ground—that was music."

All these minds we today describe as civilized were silent in the presence of the body so as to capture its vibrations. They extolled this movement but now we sway our bodies only to melodies. For Hilda, this was very, very bad.

"Only when dance overcomes music, when it tames it, does it become dance."

"Why don't you say that they are inherently linked?"

"That's how life is. There always has to be a victor and a vanquished."

"Conflict?"

"Competition. To bring out the best in us. Listen, it's like men and women. When they simply exist alongside each other, neither of them arouses the other's interest."

"Does there always have to be conflict, darling?"

"No, not conflict. But they have to conceal some things from each other, so you keep looking at your partner and feeling that there is still more to discover about him, even if he is exposed before you, totally naked but with thousands of outfits he hasn't worn yet but that you are eager to see him in. So that things don't end. Right?

"Things don't end. We simply stop seeing their radiance."

"But isn't the climax when dance and music become one?"

"I don't know, maybe. Perhaps they can't come together like that."

"Isn't life complete when a man and woman become one? When he penetrates her, he fills something inside her. Listen, if it weren't for this coupling there would be no conception. There would be no childbirth."

"Maybe you're right, but at a given moment they go back to being apart. He goes back to being a man and she goes back to being a woman. Maybe music doesn't want to be a simply a tool for dance, and maybe dance doesn't want to need melodies to complement it."

"But the moment they come together, they become an artistic tableau."

Then Hilda smiled, perhaps not as an indication that she was convinced but to express her happiness at the conversation. I too loved talking with her about everything. I loved our disagreements, our debates, our conversations, our questioning each other only to prompt new questions. Like Shahrazad's mesmerizing tales, we always left ours open-ended in the same way. At those moments, we were like New York and all the cities that never sleep.

I don't know what happened to this spark and how our love dried up, nor how I transformed from a classy lover to a total failure. I don't know what instinct pushes a person—man or woman—to exchange that spark with apprehension and fear. Perhaps it is just daily concerns that make a man, for example, forget why he loves his wife and why he got together with her in the first place. Perhaps it's the same instinct that pushes a woman to stop seeing the man she loves the way she did upon her first impression.

Why do relationships always start with amazement and end with apathy and lethargy? Is this human nature? A lack of honesty? Boredom? Why do lovers stop being interested in each other after shorter or longer periods, depending on circumstances? Why does love always seem to have an expiration date, as if it were doomed never to be renewed? Do passion and perseverance disappear when a relationship is revived? Do great relationships really become better after time passes, and is this a premonition of eternal love?

I don't know why I can't believe that the most beautiful part of love is its beginning, like most people do. Where are the details that create this beauty? "Love is the continual exercise of loving," Hilda used to tell me. "It doesn't abandon us—we are the ones who must create it."

She always used to ask me if I would stay with her if she fell ill some day, if I would be with her however bad it was. Now, with the time long passed since I should have told her my answer, I knew what it was. I knew I should have told her that even the worst thing about her would elicit my desire.

Isn't a woman's topography what her body makes familiar? Isn't this the difference? I didn't tell her how much I loved to touch her hair or how much I loved her rebelliousness—so much that I feared it being used against me—or how much I sometimes desired to touch her lips with my fingers and could keep touching them for hours. I didn't tell her that afterward I would go back and recall everything about her: the size of her breasts, the length of her fingers, and even the shape of her back and abdominal muscles. I didn't tell her that all these things made her and that I wanted to have her back with me so much.

I also wanted her to knock at my door, to beg me to let her come back to me, not because of pride but to be sure of her love for me. Why didn't she write in her letters to me that she would die without me? Why didn't she die without me? Why didn't she tell me that she was suffering like I was suffering? Why did she insist on these letters being a kind of diary of her daily life—and why did they suddenly stop coming? Why wasn't there one last, pleading letter? Why?

"Perhaps you aren't so different from the people you labeled your 'executioners' during the war. You are like them, waiting for a scourge to ruin our love. Damn you, damn them, and damn everything else too."

Why were these your last, cruel words?

"My dear Hilda, I am not like them. I am still waiting for you to come back one day. I am still waiting to hear your little hands knocking on my door...."

I started writing this letter, but just as quickly erased every word. I couldn't say this to her. I didn't want to arouse her pity. Perhaps she really did see me as like them, a brutal predator, and because of that she didn't want to understand my enormous love.

I immersed myself in my computer screen, hesitating between writing another letter or forgetting everything when the telephone rang. By the time I could answer, the caller had left a voice message.

Hilda, it's Eva.... I've been trying to reach you on your cell phone for a while but it's switched off. I wanted to meet for a coffee. I know I've been really distant recently. I changed my phone number after splitting up with Mike and didn't tell you ... but there's a lot to talk about. I really miss you. Please call me back at this number: 917 293 1075. I'm waiting for your call. Kisses.

I called Eva back at the number she left. I wanted to be close to something or someone that reminded me of Hilda and that felt like a bridge between us.

"Hello, Eva? This is Majd, how are you?"

"Hi, Majd. I'm well, how about you?"

"I'm OK. I found your message. Hilda isn't here. She went to Beirut."

"Oh, really? When?"

"A few months ago."

"Why? Are you two OK?"

"I don't know. She's not here."

"Listen, Majd, what's her number in Beirut?"

"I don't know."

"You aren't calling her?"

"It's hard to explain."

"Where are you right now?"

"At home."

"Can you meet me for a coffee?"

"Yes."

"I'm on Fifth Avenue. I'll wait for you at Empire Café."

"Great, I'm coming."

As I drove to the café we agreed to meet at I kept thinking about America, this place of legends that enchants Americans and foreigners alike. I saw its largest city, New York, as a city of opposites, and it really is. If you compare Broadway and Fifth Avenue, which intersect in Times Square, you feel that you have moved from one world to another in a matter of minutes.

Everything in the city seems full: its material well-being and its seemingly endless, diverse sources of wealth, from the automobile industry to the industry of Hollywood movies. And it doesn't end there. New York always seems to me also to be on the brink of the abyss, as if all this unfettered speed and progress in urbanization must end like an ancient Greek tragedy. I used to always ask myself where all this power was going: to its ascent or its fall? For me it was like the picture of a mighty man who is unaware of his fate.

Is it possible that one spot on the world map can bring everything together? That there is a place where some curricula are superficial but others have depth? A country where people in the North are industrialists and Southerners adhere to their traditions? Perhaps this is the reason for the power of the United States, that it's a puzzling enigma—like a river that has many tributaries but one outlet.

As much as I loved this country, I begrudged it and hated its power. A country with this much power can't be compassionate; this is perhaps why I used to feel that we Arabs and Palestinians were this country's fuel.

I always felt that I was closer to Broadway than Fifth Avenue. Broadway was a filthy, winding street. Whenever I crossed it, I felt that electric currents were coursing through me because of the intensity of its speed. Its cheap restaurants were noisy and full of people of so many backgrounds. As they walked, passersby could hear the clanging of people's knives and forks. I always used to see men with solitude on their faces and middle-aged women endlessly chatting.

To me it seemed like the underworld street par excellence; I always used to ask why the most important New York theater was located on one of its cheapest streets. Is it because the theater is a people's showcase, making us see the essence of ordinary people? This street hides thugs and criminals in its recesses, and its refuse is practically a breeding ground for them. Its cheap things, its cheap emotions—all of them seem real. The streets have skin and flesh as well. The body of Broadway here is in a state of continual flow. This is the face of America, overcrowded with inhabitants, with everything: values and the lack of values, morals and the lack of morals, love and the absence of love.

After you cross toward Fifth Avenue, you feel that you are meeting a new America. Here is where you find its harsh side. Its capitalist side, where there's no room for the poor or the rest of the world. There's no room for failures and countries at a lower level. There's arrogance, intransigence, and the exaggerated formulas that the American authorities use in their speeches to present their country as invincible and a never-ending dream. Fifth Avenue is an aristocratic street shimmering with cleanliness; its inhabitants are New York's remaining dignitaries. Towering buildings. The most expensive entertainments are sold there and the most powerful human temptations. Straight, orderly, colorless indifference, except for those who come with a lot of money or a lot of beauty. It's a street that takes mercy on no one, like all the places where there's no end to human misery. There are international brands and the very finest dining. It's where Eva found herself queen of the world. How else could it be when it lifted her from rock bottom to the very top? Who could resist the temptations of the super rich, if they were not immune to opulence? Why did he resist it?

I got to the café and found Eva waiting for me. She got up from her chair and came over to me, planting a kiss on my cheek. She had on a lot of makeup and bright red lipstick. She was wearing skinny jeans and a black top that accentuated her big breasts. But she was alluring and beautiful. A woman who has lots of treasures inside her and desire pouring from her eyes, one of those women who can call out to you without saying one word. This was the first time I looked at Eva with the eyes of a man who didn't know her. I wasn't in thrall of her, but I suddenly noticed a concentration of details about her, or perhaps because on that day she had gone to great effort to take care of her appearance.

"I see that you have gotten more beautiful."

She laughed and brought her glass of water to her still-smiling lips.

Women always need to hear flattery and compliments.

"You, madame, are gorgeous."

She laughed again. But suddenly her features turned serious, as if she were practicing for a role as an actress. "So now, tell me, where is Hilda? What's going on with you two?"

"Fine.... A while ago, Hilda decided to go back to Beirut. She didn't give a specific date for her return. And communication between us stopped."

"What do you mean that communication between the two of you stopped? Just like that? So easily? You two were in love like the stuff of romance novels...."

"I do not know, my friend. I don't know what took her over there."

"Don't you miss her?"

I was silent. What to answer?

"What's gotten into you? God? Do you miss her?"

"Yes, I miss her a lot."

"What is this nonsense, then? Why aren't you speaking to her?"

"I don't want to."

"You're so childish. Give me her number. I'll speak to her."

"Listen Eva. My relationship with Hilda is impossible. Yes, impossible. She is South and I am West. She is North and I am East. She is fire and I am water. She's over there and I'm not anywhere. She dances and I can barely move my leg."

"But you two are in love with each other."

"She's that distant thing you can't beg me to capture. Do you think I don't love her? I adore her, but I know we have to be apart. There is that ancient past between us. Not because I care about it so much but because they won't ever accept me. For her I am a part of a bitter past, and she is the same for me. Not she herself but all of the things that happened in the past. Do you understand what I'm saying?"

"I don't understand. Or maybe I do. But I don't agree."

"We'd grown more distant … even in the last period when we were together. There was a chasm between us I don't understand. I felt afraid to go near her. There are so many things I can't explain or understand. Now every day I try to get used to the idea that Hilda is gone and find some moments with her that were real and true."

"Can you leave those moments aside easily?"

"No, I can't put them aside. They are reality."

"I don't understand.... I, for example, left my despicable boyfriend because of his serial cheating. There was a tangible reason, an end. Can you stand for there not to be a reason for your love ending?"

"I can't, at least not now. But perhaps with time I'll be able to."

"Listen, Majd, I know I'm not the best person to give you advice. For a long time my life was a total mess, but I know I can't leave aside happiness so easily. If I found something that made me happy, I would cleave onto it with my very teeth. Sometimes I bite into it so hard for fear of losing it that I harm it. I'm aware I'm doing this so I can then go back and hold onto it more gently. What if you were doing that without realizing it? Biting into Hilda with your teeth?"

"But she's biting, too.... And she's not here anymore...."

In my conversation with Eva I felt like a man stripped of his solid foundations, as if I had been completely laid bare in front of her. I wasn't mighty like the street we were on. I wasn't solid. Just brittle. Perhaps it was her strength that brought out my weakness. She was one of those women who you can't deceive or lie to. You can't feign indifference, because she would consider your lack of interest as a grave offence and hold you accountable. My look of brokenheartedness—because I'd lost the woman I loved—betrayed me. It was possible to conceal from most people the frustration I felt, but not from her.

Eva interrupted my silence, telling me I had to speak to Hilda. I found myself on the verge of tears when faced with her insistence.

"Listen, don't be stupid. Don't neglect your feelings because of fear and delusions. Go to her. Speak to her. Tell her how much you want her."

"But you don't know. I can't just do that. Look at me, Eva, really look. You see a successful man before you, living on a street like this one we are sitting on, but do you see what I have concealed inside myself? Do you know how many times I've had to go against my own body to be living like Fifth Avenue? Do you know that behind me I'm hiding Broadway and all the debris that's crammed into it? What can I give her? My defeat? A homeland I don't know? American citizenship that I don't feel reflects who I am? "

"I don't know why you have to mix all these things together and squeeze love in the middle of it."

"Well, were you able to separate your past from your present, my friend?"

Eva didn't answer. We weren't here to compete about whose past was worse. We were strangers in a city that brought us together because it didn't know our secrets. We were here because in New York we were able, or we thought we were able, to be anonymous, to walk in the streets and not see the faces of the past. No one who looked at Eva, the actress from Mexico, knew that she was a girl who ran away from her mother's husband and his violation of her body.

"I do this because I want a good and happy life."

"Won't my life be miserable without love?"

"Listen Majd, I'm not Hilda. I'm not a girl who ran away from an aristocratic family whose biggest problem was an excess of kindness. I am a woman bred in the earth's soil, its dirt, its sweat. But I know how she feels. I know the meaning of a person being alone. I know the meaning of taking refuge in someone and thinking that he will bring you justice and help you see locked doors. I know denial. And because I know all of this I know very well that I can identify things that are good and right. You and Hilda are that. You suit one another.

When she was talking, I felt for a moment that I understood why I loved Hilda. For moments Eva was no longer that woman who aborted babies but a good, wise woman.

"I want to ask you one thing: did you really abort Mohsen's baby?"

"What if I did?"

"I just want to know."

"I'm not going to tell you."

"Are you really sleeping with a woman now?"

"Why are you putting your nose in my private life now?"

"I want to know."

"What do you want me to say? No, I didn't have an abortion and no, I'm not a lesbian? If I answer like that will you feel better? Listen Majd, do you know my story? Do you know it?"

Damn this woman. Why wasn't she troubled by my answers? Why did she take everything at its word? Why didn't she break down and cry and tell me that she really did have an abortion, and that she regretted that she was with women because her image of men became so distorted? Why did she insist on being so tenacious—even more tenacious than me?

"Listen, would it help you to know that I get drunk on wine every night to forget my tragedy, that my insides are crushed? But that's not reality. I used to be like that years ago and cry every time I talked about my past. But then something changed. I don't know if it was me or time. But I am not that broken, violated woman. I cast off that image."

Eva kept on talking. She said that when she first left home when young, she knew she didn't want anyone's pity, that she wanted to hold on to her right to happiness. She told me that when she took refuge with her father after the rape, he didn't say a thing about it and acted as if he didn't care.

"There was sadness and suffering in my mother's eyes. Loss mixed with harshness. That loss perhaps made me forgive her but there was no empathy in my father's gaze. He said nothing. What did you expect me to feel? I started curling myself up like a ball in my bed every night, wrapping up in my body waiting for my stepfather to assault me, like I was ready to be raped. Every night I swore that I wouldn't ever have children. I got pregnant by him. I aborted the baby. I kept jumping on the bed until it tired of me flailing around, and my mother came in to find me covered in blood. I could see death. I decided to leave after that. I didn't have a specific destination; I landed up in New York because a man in Mexico wanted me to become a prostitute here. I let him believe it so I could cross to the other side, and I did cross. Then I ran away from him. I stole his money before leaving. I started working in a nail salon. I put polish on stupid American ladies' fingernails. But I wanted a better life. I befriended men and they spent lots of money to be with me. I chose the less attractive ones because they don't have self-confidence and will pay a lot for women's company to compensate for their ugliness. Sometimes I also felt I was fond of them. But this love was coupled with personal self-gratification—that is, I loved them as long as I was getting what I wanted. I didn't cry at night for my useless honor, nor over superstitions and nonsense that we expect from women who opt out of traditional understandings of love and giving. I didn't think about redemption. I used to think that I saved money to feel secure. But whenever I saved up some money I wanted more. It was my heaven and my hell at the same time. Then I found Mike.

"Things changed with him. I loved him. I loved him as much as he took care of me. But he came home with the smell of other women on him and I would cry. I would really cry. I don't know if it was because of this or because I felt that I was a woman who could be replaced. I used to think that I was the most beautiful, strongest, and most exciting woman but then I saw him leave all this for other women. I tried to stay with him, to forget about it. But I was really deeply destroyed. I was honest with him; I told him about my tragedies. I don't know why he wasn't good to me. I used to think that he would make up for everything. Afterward I went down the path of revenge, but it ended with me kicking the other man out of my bed right after I finished with him. I was destroyed. I thought about leaving every day but I didn't know if I could be without all the luxury I'd been immersed in. I didn't know if it was linked to money even. I used to want to hold onto Mike in any way possible, to make him stop cheating and come back to me, to tell me he hadn't found another woman like me. Perhaps I stayed because of this.

"I didn't get pregnant by him. Don't worry. I didn't ever stop taking birth control pills. My promise to myself to never get pregnant was stronger than any desire for or illusion of love. When I left, I only hoped for all of this to stop—my love, my hatred, my anger, my desire to be his sole passion. I felt exhausted, that I was merely content as it was, and I wanted to forget everything. But I also used to want to make him suffer, too, to make him taste my confusion and my anguish, to feel that I had beaten him. So I invented the story of the baby. He's your friend. You can now tell him that there wasn't any baby. My game's over."

I didn't ask Eva why her game was over now, and why she wanted to free herself from the vicious circle that she was stuck in. Perhaps she wanted to free herself from Mike, too, but no longer cared if he was hurting or not. Her desire to end the game with a new beginning shone in her eyes. And she had found a new world—acting. She said that she had now started to feel as though the world recognized her as a star, that she had become someone important—as she had dreamed of becoming to compensate for her previous losses.

Eva put her hand over her mouth to prevent the conversation from continuing, as if she felt for a second that she'd said more than she should have. I didn't ask her if she and her producer were really in love, as rumored. She was very transparent and more generous than necessary in her revelations.

She stayed like that. Her hand over her mouth. Her eyes filled with tears. "My grandmother used to say, 'They will oppress you and no one will help you escape injustice. They won't admit that they oppressed you. This is the fate of beautiful girls.' She knew."

A little smile emerged from among Eva's tears. I tried to go over to her and hug her and calm her fears. Her other hand let me know that I should stay seated. She took my hand and told me, "For those of us who have only rarely known it, happiness is accompanied by a huge fear of losing it. I am really very happy right now. I don't know what these tears are, but I will tell you just one thing—being freed from suffering is a great feeling, and those of us who have spent our lives walking on thorns deserve it. Don't give up on Hilda. I'm already late now but I'm really glad to have met up with you, my friend."

Eva bade me farewell, leaving me stunned and confused. Should I pick up the phone, call Mohsen, and tell him that there was no baby? Should I go and send Hilda a letter telling her that she was my chance for happiness? Nothing. I wouldn't do a thing. I asked for the bill. I paid it and then went home.

-7-

Mayhem. That's what afflicted me after my conversation with Eva. I could see an image of her stepfather raping her. I could hear one slap after another bombarding her face. I could see him putting his penis in her mouth and her crying. Image after image and my chest tightening.

We children of the massacre were like her, I thought—covered in blood no one can wash away. "You take refuge in someone thinking he will help you.... He won't even admit that he harmed you." Her words rang in my ears. No one helps anyone in this stupid life. You only extend your hand in the middle of the mud to lift your body and run away. All these delusions that we have about justice in the West, aren't they only justice built on other peoples' dead bodies?

Isn't America built on the land of dead indigenous people? But they triumphed. They created a legend. They became a legend. What did we do other than write long poems to the dead? We picked up weapons. We were dispersed. We scattered. We pointed our guns at each other. The world abandoned us. We started begging for our state. What's right was lost. What now?

Mayhem. Eva's violated body. I could smell its fragrance when I was near her while she was talking. Her only triumph was the luxury she now lived in, but her body was still exhausted. Time hadn't healed it. She triumphed in luxury, as I did by becoming a businessman whose office was on the ninety-ninth floor. The view from up so high was really different and it was also deceptive. For a long time it made me feel that I was a man in whom nothing was broken. But I remained a man without a homeland.

The Americans are always standing on top of the world, controlling it with their fingers. What pleasure is there in all this power? Their people are driven by the current carrying them, not carried along by empty slogans like we Arabs are. They are driven forward because their lives are good and untouched by hatred. If they had their rights stolen from them like we had, would they have been able to go ahead?

Mayhem. Eva's body faded and Hilda's body came into focus. A youthful, new body. Soft and gentle. How many times did I tear into that body? How many times did I cram it between my thighs to diminish it, pulling on her head? How many times did she moan when under me, screaming, "I want you to take me now"? How many times did her screams enrapture me while she was begging me to take her? Nothing arouses a man's desire more than a crazy woman desiring him. Her orgasm ended in laughter that captured the very essence of all life. I would smile and listen to it ringing throughout the apartment.

I went in the room where she used to practice dancing. I saw Martha Graham's picture that she'd hung on the middle of the wall.

"Who is that woman, Hilda?"

"Martha."

"Martha who? Should I know her?"

"Martha Graham. She is the inventor of modern dance. An incredible woman. Do you think that this is the best place for the picture or should I move it to another wall?"

"No, it seems good here."

Hilda laughed that day. She told me about Graham and how she had started her journey in dance. "Do you know that contemporary dance came as a reaction to the monotony of ballet? While seeking a space for free movement. Ballet doesn't appeal to me. Perhaps it has its own charm, but I hate everything so bounded by rules." Hilda would move her hands while talking. She told me about the many dances Graham had choreographed. She said that she had been generous and didn't go after anyone when they borrowed from or were inspired by her choreography. "I've loved this woman since I was young.... I read about her."

She told me that Graham had been married and was madly in love and then suffered from depression as she grew older. "She saw everything through the dances she had danced with her husband. She used to see other people dancing them and cry. She missed him. I don't know how a man could leave a woman like her ... but she came back. As if coming back from the dead."

For a long time Hilda seemed like a cluster of passion whenever she talked. Continual, fiery fervor. Enthusiastic. Yielding to the flames. I'll admit that all of this made me afraid that she didn't love like ordinary women, women who cook dinner for their men and wait for them at home to come back from the café.

To love an unconventional woman is very dangerous, because you feel that your manhood is at risk. It's not like the normal workings of masculinity. Such a woman doesn't need a man like so many women need their husbands—to keep unruly children in line or to ask for money for the household expenses, for example. She isn't with him to show off in front of her friends or family. Indeed, Hilda was different. How to explain her presence in my life? I could find nothing to account for it but love. It was difficult to believe that love could just be there like that, without any social pressure.

She used to tell me I was her friend and lover, but was that enough to make her stay with me or, in other words, to make her stay forever? She was free, and this bothered me. That is why her going to Beirut seemed such a big threat. Was I doomed to her fleeing me some day?

I closed the door to the room quietly and lay down to sleep. That night I was no longer afraid of what would happen. Perhaps because of Eva's words and a desire to imitate them. "You can now tell him that there wasn't any baby." With that, I knew that she was free of Mike. That night, I no longer wanted to punish Hilda for going away. I no longer wanted to take a confrontational stance: me against them. I only wanted to embrace Hilda until we both fell asleep. I didn't want to wait for her to knock at my door to be convinced that love would triumph over everything.

Did love do all of this to me? Could it become a homeland? I do not know.

-8-

When Marianne got the phone call from an American Army officer, inviting her into the office, she thought the reason was her constant criticism of America's involvement in the Gulf War. It never occurred to her that closure was awaiting her in a sealed envelope.

"I barely said hello and sat down in his office when I looked at him defiantly as if I were trying to say that I wouldn't go back on my opposition to our participation in the war. He didn't ask me my opinion. He spoke directly to me saying that they had found human remains in Iraq and afterward had done DNA tests on them, comparing them to samples taken from John's relatives. The results turned out to be identical.

"Ma'am, your husband died many years ago. We found the body in the desert in Kuwait. I am very sorry for your loss; your husband died, sacrificing himself in duty for his country. Please accept our deepest condolences."

"Remains. The body. Where is John?"

This is how she answered the American officer. She didn't say more than that. Marianne said that she was searching for closure, but when the officer told her, she felt that time stopped.

"I don't know why I didn't cry.... He's been dead for years and I didn't know. And when I did know I didn't cry."

News of a loved one's death happens like a vacuum in the soul, and sometimes it is such a huge shock that you can't even manage to cry. People often can't explain their reactions. Tragedy is somehow outside their scope of comprehension.

In Marianne's case, everything happened so quickly—war, death, loss. But time stops with dead bodies left in the sand, so many questions and doubts. Her suffering increased each day with the kind of confusion that leaves a person wide open, standing on the edge of the abyss. She stood on the edge for years until her body was numb, and when she finally fell, death didn't shake her. It was completely still, and years would pass before she would become fully aware of it.

From that time on, my American friend became a very calm woman. No, not exactly calm but simply silent. It wasn't so much the death that affected her but what came afterward, the days that passed amid the sense of absence that confirmation of her loss brought, especially since it had been such a premature loss. She was experiencing that strength which turns such a person's life upside down, which changes him or her either into a rebellious revolutionary or a hermit who withdraws from the world.

Marianne's bed officially opened itself to all possibilities. She was able to have anyone she wanted in it and build a new relationship: she could start to love again without hanging onto the possibility that John was still alive. But was this possible? Why, even after she was sure he was dead, did she keep thinking that she was betraying the memory she held of her husband?

Even at her husband's funeral, Marianne seemed to act as if he'd died suddenly. She delivered a painful speech that day:

> *My dear John,*
>
> *I do not know if you are able to hear me now, and I also don't know if we can speak to the dead. You were alone in a strange land, fighting a battle I wasn't convinced about then. Perhaps if you had listened to me, you would have stayed here when all that happened. Perhaps at your funeral it is also shameful for me to hold you accountable and say that I asked you not to go. But, my dear husband, forgive me; your terrible loss prevents me from following the rules of humanity, love, and compassion. I can't simply just tolerate your absence. I can't be that strong person who believes that everything happens for a reason. I can't do this while I feel that I am in dire need of you every day, I can't do this when I look in my children's faces and know that their father is gone. Yes, life goes on, but it isn't like it was when you were here. I love you.*

Everyone at the funeral cried at his wife's speech except her. But when I heard her voice saying those words, I could imagine knives scratching at her throat and body. She went over to his grave, put the rest of the flowers on it, and made the sign of the cross. Then she walked back with slow, heavy footsteps, as a person does at a difficult farewell.

-8-

When I opened my email the next day, I found a message from my cousin Muhammad. It was about his girlfriend, Mariam. And it was the first time he had sent me something so long.

> *Mariam has gotten married. The shutters of the windows I used to look at her through remained closed for more than a week. I almost went mad. I asked everyone about her. No one would tell me anything. I went to her brother's shop and we quarreled. He hit me, I hit him back. He told me he was going to register a complaint against me with the police if he saw me near his shop or home again. Only yesterday they opened the shutters. I saw many women in the room. They were all wearing white. I came right up to the window when she was alone with her sister in the room. She looked at me and closed the shutters. I want to go and beat everyone up. But I stayed in my room. I listened to the honking of car horns. I didn't look at her when she left the building. I could only hear the happy sounds of the wedding. Terrible sounds. The camp never seemed so bleak to me before. This was*

the sound of joy. Women's faces in Mariam's room, thick makeup on their cheeks and lips. What is this wedding that happened after only one or two weeks? Some miserable man living abroad came and took her. A relative of theirs who lived in Africa. That's all I knew. I didn't try to see them. I preferred he remain a featureless man who took my girlfriend, hoping it would lighten the brunt of the loss. Surely you are thinking: what is this love that happens behind the shutters, and you think that I am stupid. But this is love here in the camp. A girl, closed shutters, and disappointment. Probably it's not at all what love looks like for Americans. I was waiting for this to happen for long days and months, and the strange thing is that when it did happen, I was calm. Don't laugh. But, really, surrendering in my own room was my way of accepting the defeat. Perhaps now I will stop looking at Mariam's window. Don't ask me why I chose to write about this to you in particular. Perhaps if I had gone to sit with the rest of the guys here I would have become the object of everyone's ridicule. You're far away. Perhaps the fact that you can't see all this me makes it easier for me to expose my embarrassment to you in this way. The guys here in the camp have good hearts. They get together here in the courtyard every day, smoke argilehs and light fires to roast potatoes and chestnuts. This is how they battle boredom. Everyone also smokes weed. Not me. The other guys. I don't know if this kind of get-together would interest you. Write to me about New York. How do young people pass their time over there?

I smiled while reading my cousin's letter. It was so spontaneous and full of innocence. I didn't know what to tell him. I had paternal feelings toward him, so I found myself inviting him to New York:

Dear Muhammad,

Don't be sad about this girl's marriage. No one knows what is written in our fate. What do you think about coming to visit me here in New York? What if you tried to get a visa for the United States? I could pay for your ticket and trip. We could see how to arrange things and get the required documents. That way you could see New York up close. Love, Majd

His answer came the very same evening:

Do you mean what you are saying? This is like a dream come true for me. I will get the papers together. I can't even tell you how thrilled I am. I feel like I've been reborn.

I wanted to reach out to my cousin and all those people for whom luck had determined that my life would be better than their lives. I remembered my father and his continual recommendations to the people around us, never to cut their ties with those still in the camps. He used to say that he was well aware of their suffering. "All of them say, Palestine, Palestine, no one loves Palestine," he used to repeat, disappointed. "Well, if they really loved it enough they wouldn't have let her be lost.".

Why is it always easier to talk about suffering than to do something about it? As humans do we actually have to see another person's suffering to act? Is there any joy in the fact that there are always victims in life, victims we feel superior to, and that we see our own burdens as less stressful? Was my father right? Are we Palestinians a detested people? If not, why don't the Arab countries open their doors to welcome us in?

Are we an ungrateful people? Why are we a people always seen only as "a people"? Isn't it possible for there to be good Palestinians and bad Palestinians?

Outwardly, most people claim to sympathize with our cause. But what do they say behind the scenes? They transform us into individuals stigmatized by hostility and individuals it's easy to accuse of anything because they are homeless. Even our imaginary heroism, which some people claim for us, only trades on our suffering. If everyone meant what they said about how much they loved the Palestinians, we would have found ourselves rulers of the kingdom. But the world doesn't owe us the liberation of our homeland. The world can barely manage to give us a tent, a mattress, and sheets. We must take it upon ourselves. We must find another way out.

I wanted to ask Muhammad to leave everything behind but I knew that even if I arranged for him to live here for a while, it wouldn't be possible. His first impression of America would bother him. So too, he would realize that we Palestinians are a people doomed to the past, because without it we have lost any hope of existing at all. We possess unknown fates, we live on the margins despite our existence in the center of life. We hope to create another past. But at the same time we keep hanging on to our memory, clinging to the hope of returning.

Part Four

-I-

Hilda

Deciding after a long absence to step foot on the land you were born in demands a lot of courage. You don't just return to your memory and that's it, but you exhume it, searching for what's right and wrong. This was my problem throughout my life—my lack of ability to accept things as they were. Perhaps if I had been able to be this "I" that I was supposed to be, things would have been much easier. Perhaps.

Sitting in the window seat on the airplane, I looked at the clouds, which seemed like a mattress I could throw myself on top of and make my home on forever. But then it occurred to me that this white bed was delusive, like a homeland, because if I dared to discover whether it was merely an overcast sky, it would surely let me plummet straight through it to the ground.

I know you're very angry I came back, perhaps fearing you'd lose me. But if you had thought a little bit about how much I love you, you would have understood that this return was necessary. There are people who leave their countries to escape, and I don't want to be one of them. I don't want to uproot myself and become a new woman. I want only to know why I left and if an eventual return here one day would be impossible.

When you go against your roots, something strange happens to you. You are shaken. You sometimes imagine that even the shape of your body has changed as if you took it out of the mold so it would become another size. This painful labor is a journey into the unknown. At times you don't know why you took it or if it was even a decision. It's like dancing. You have to go deep into your body. You have to abandon it completely in order to become more aware of it. You don't become a good dancer by chance, you become one because you endured the pain, which constant dancing demands, to become able to take charge of your body, to be able to bend your limbs with flexibility and suppleness and without pain.

While practicing, something forced me to challenge myself, as if I believed that there was another body, or even bodies, waiting for me. Believing that if I broke the first barrier, no others would be able to defeat me. When you leave the way you were first molded, you feel liberated.

After so much exhaustion and suffering, you feel like someone sitting at home on the balcony. The wind hits you and you smell freedom. You smile at the thought that you have transformed your body into a canvas.

I gave myself over to this art. It was my salvation. I used to want life to be there, on the stage with music. That way my return to Lebanon would be less daunting, I figured, because when I wanted to go back to New York I would not lack options.

I was able to face things, settle accounts, and condemn, but I wasn't here for that. I was here so I could understand. I was here because of you, too, Majd. I wanted to know if I loved you because of your injuries, because I wanted to prove that I was an affectionate and generous woman. Or if I actually loved you because we were truly in love without there being a reason why. I also returned because I used to be afraid of returning. And because I was afraid to tell you that you—if you decided to keep taking only parts of me—would reproduce the kinds of reasons that made me leave here to begin with.

Suffering sometimes gives us the feeling that we are permitted to do anything, that we are entitled to take revenge on everything, to demolish things merely for the sake of demolition. It prevents us from asking ourselves where we have erred. Suffering is temptation. Temptation is what makes you hold onto your crippled leg and the scar on your face. Temptation doesn't want to heal from tragedy.

You always anticipated the end of our love, as if you wanted to control it with death. Indeed, you held to your conviction that I would leave you, completing your tragedy. But I am neither America nor a stand-in for Zionism. I am a woman who used to want to be with you, I memorized all your details: the smell of your clothes, how you like your morning coffee.

When I was in New York, you used to miss my performances, to refuse to come to see me dance. At the beginning, guilty as I felt about your physical state, I made excuses for your not attending. But one day your absence made me so sad that I started to cry. Eva told me, "Hilda, are you asking for your boyfriend's forgiveness for feeling as you do rather than God's forgiveness? Asking this of either of them isn't fair to them or to you."

Eva said this because, as she saw it, I'd suffered from not telling you clearly that I couldn't excuse your absence. I know that it's hard for you to stare into your face and free it from the scar. I know that it is hard for you because your tragedy has never ended, and you feel that removing the wound would mean removing the truth. I used to only want you to transcend a few things for my sake, to believe that I love you like this regardless of anything.

There is a side of me that you know very well: the cheerful girl who laughs and dances. But there is another side, one you force me to see when you ask me to look at my body in the mirror. There are flashes of light through the darkness, there is skin spitting out the pain.

All of this made me question myself. I grew up with you. I matured. I perhaps became a woman and wanted to go back to see my past with the eyes of an adult. This woman contained both your tragedy and mine. Reburying that part of her without letting her gaze at her features—that is, without letting her and even encouraging her to return—was perhaps an unforgiveable crime.

You know hardly a thing about the place that I came from. If I showed your picture to the members of my family, it would perhaps be impossible for me to be accepted here anymore. I am a part of the ruling system, from a people who basked in the glory of family and the party.

We—and here I exclude myself as Hilda, and address her simply as a part of this entity imposed on her—are an Orthodox Christian family from the Metn region in

Lebanon, this vast homeland that one day we felt should be ours alone and we would fight and kill for.

I lived my entire life with the pictures of my ancestors, the most important men of the village, chasing me. It's like the curse of the ninety-ninth floor that you used to feel. These heights are very tempting, but they prevent you from coming close to real life. I was one of those special girls whom a driver dropped off at school and whose father knew the teachers and the nuns who in turn held the utmost respect for him.

I never knew the pain of the people in the camps, the people you told me about, nor were any of my life choices narrow or virtually nonexistent. Those people you talked about were always our subordinates, strangers.

I used to go to church every day, walking behind my mother, until I caught up to her. I used to watch her praying to our Lord Jesus and I did as she did. My existence as a Christian girl gave me a sense of being close to God. In this space inside the church you felt that you could be closer or further from the altar, speak to Jesus directly, and ask for forgiveness.

Others inhabited a strange world we didn't know a thing about. If some of the girls in school hadn't spoken about Muslims, I wouldn't have known there were other religions than my own. I don't know why I feel that I am writing a letter of introduction about myself to a man I spent more than two years with. He should have started to get to know me.

But do you know that in New York I wasn't this spoiled Christian girl? That I became just Hilda? My story sounds so foolish, as a narration about the burden of luxury being so distant from reality. But no. I had my share of unhappiness. In this cocoon in which I lived, everything was measured.

Exorbitant prices. The father who considers himself and his family better than everything else. The father who bestowed his love on his younger daughter—me—at the expense of her older sister, who almost ruined the family's reputation in the village.

I never told you about my sister Mathilde. It's not because I'm ashamed of her, not at all, but because I lost some of my sisterly feelings for her. Nor do you know that my sister doesn't love me. It's not right to say that she doesn't love me, but let's say that I'm her rival of sorts. There's a huge crack, a gap between us, not caused by a stranger. Perhaps my father did it unintentionally. And again I say "perhaps."

The women here used to describe Mathilde as the most beautiful young woman ever. Her big blue eyes were like stars shining in the night sky. Her light brown skin was as soft as a sandy beach, and her wavy blond hair reached halfway down her back. When the old people in the village talked about beauty they would use Mathilde as an example, but this description was always followed by a deep sigh. "What heartbreak she has brought us," was the lament I swore I heard more than a hundred times about my sister, who was twelve years older than me.

I remember that when I was young I used to see Mathilde as one of the gods we read about in legends or the heroines in fairy tales—the glamorous Cinderella, Sleeping Beauty, or Rapunzel. My sister was a bit of all of them, the exemplar of what I wanted to be like when I grew up. I also imitated her: I wore her clothes when she wasn't there and I put on her captivating perfumes.

There was charisma there, at least one of a sort that enchanted me. The fairy tale girl whose room I shared. I watched her comb her long hair, which looked like a cascading waterfall, and sometimes I asked her to comb mine like hers. She was very good to me, and even if we didn't play together, because of our age difference, she was still playful and affectionate.

Mathilde occupied a particular position at home in my father's heart. He was as proud of her as he was of his gun and his land. She was also fully immersed in life: she danced, sang, and laughed. Sometimes she also drank beer or wine with the grown-ups. She learned how to drive. She was preparing to enter university and to travel to finish her studies abroad because of the situation in Lebanon.

She had a lot of friends—boys and girls. Some men who used to visit her were also fighters in the party. She wore short skirts and tight shirts. She was my window to the world. Many times I would stuff tissues in my bra so my breasts would be as big as hers, and I too wore red lipstick, so my lips would be cherry-colored like hers. She was almost everything.

Suddenly long nights passed with Mathilde's bed empty. I woke up and cried from loneliness. On the few occasions when I would see her during this time, my sister changed toward me. She was no longer kind and gentle like before. She became something else, and I couldn't understand what.

It wasn't long before my sister's bed disappeared from her room. Some workers took it out. With only one bed remaining, the space was bigger. My father told me that day that the room was now mine alone, I could enjoy the big cupboard and he would put in a desk in place of Mathilde's bed. When I asked him about her, a scowl spread across his face and he asked me not to talk anymore and spoil the moment. "Use the big room. I'll fill it with new toys for you. You should be happy, Bella!"

I smiled at the time to appear happy, as Bella was supposed to be, and I was quietly pleased about the toys that my father started bringing me every day. I transformed suddenly into a girl of the utmost importance in the family. Even the piano teacher risked the bombardment to come and give me lessons, complying with my father's wishes.

I imagined that my hair was growing longer, as if it were preparing to cascade down my back like Mathilde's. Even at the time, I didn't know where my sister was hiding. She wasn't dead, since there was no funeral or receiving of mourners at the house. She changed, and then went into hiding like those mysterious girls in fairy tales who were searching for something that would turn their lives radically upside down or be gripped in the clutches of evil.

In addition to my older sister, I also had a brother who was three years older than me. Can you believe that as busy as he was, he ran in the parliamentary elections to be my father's political and party successor?

My father also wanted a ministerial post. This was the atmosphere in the village. This is what happened to former fighters in this country. Their armed dominance transformed into positions of political power.

In the beginning, my father didn't want to change his old alliances or compromise on things he wouldn't have considered even discussing in the past. Now things had changed. My brother came and went to "our Master," that enigmatic man I didn't know anything about who says that glory will come to our home through our wide open doors.

"Bella, bella! You'll be surprised by good news soon!" my father used to tell me, rubbing his hands together as if preparing to receive his prize. He repeated the same sentence along with the same hand motions whenever he finished a closed-door meeting with my brother: "There is no one better to become a minister or president than someone who sacrificed his life for the good of the homeland." He would sometimes carry little Asaad around as well, telling him, "Your grandfather will show you what glory is."

In addition to our small immediate family, we have many relatives. Uncle George, his wife, and their children lived on the top floor of the family house. Others from the family lived in the village itself, right nearby or slightly further away. Everyone knew each other, like one large residential unit extending horizontally over the village land.

But the house we shared with Uncle George's family was by far the most beautiful, like a palace. A guard stood at the black iron gate and expansive gardens surrounded it. It was forbidden for us to leave without permission or a guard when there was fierce fighting. Only Mathilde enjoyed a certain freedom when she was still with us. We used to see a lot of people coming and going—most of them armed.

The other people in the village inundated us with gifts: some of them sent cooked or dried figs, others sent homemade molasses. Women brought rose water for my mother and asked her to taste their homemade products, as if it were a competition.

"Have a taste, Madame Mary. Whose molasses is more delicious, mine or Suaad's?"

My mother was always eager to please everyone, and she praised the rose water made by this person or the local kishik made by that one. After Mathilde left, my mother always made me wear my nicest clothes to meet the women who almost always came without their daughters. "By the holy cross, how beautiful this girl is," is an expression I often heard.

But when the village women came by and my mother would go in the kitchen to put their gifts into the pantry or to call on Laurice to prepare coffee for the guests and give instructions on how to serve them, I heard those other women whispering about my sister.

Their compliments would transform suddenly into gossip, and the look of wonder in their eyes would change to sharp observations. "No one sees her.... Mary doesn't know where she went.... They say she went to the madhouse in Bhannes." Each of them used to say something or other about my sister before suddenly going silent when my mother returned. The conversation would change to the war—Um Tony losing her son in battle, where things were going, the victory that was coming, East Beirut and West Beirut. Things I mostly didn't understand. I still didn't understand most of the conflicts and political parties; indeed, perhaps I preferred to know them only superficially, because all of them seemed illogical to me. I always kept my distance; I believe it was to reject all of this.

My sister's long hair alone had meaning to me amid all these horrors that we lived through. What had happened to Mathilde? Where had she disappeared? She had been off taking drugs with the party's fighters. She fell in love with a guy called Edouard. He was on pills and started sharing them with her. Not only did no one in the house notice what was going on, but they even saw no risk in her friendship with this young man.

Most of the fighters were on drugs and pills. My dad knew it, I think, but he never thought the poison could touch his own daughter's lips. He was sure that we—his son and two daughters—would never upset his image of us. For this reason his nerves were completely shattered when he learned what had become of Mathilde. Her behavior totally changed, and her complexion turned sallow. I don't know if my father and sister were speaking to each other, but according to what Laurice told me later, she was admitted to the Bhannes sanatorium after my father told his guys to force her into the car and take her to the hospital.

As Laurice once told me, "I'll never forget her face. She was like a madwoman trying to push them off of her. Her hair was swinging from side to side and she was kicking her legs up in the air. Your father was standing in the doorway motioning with his eyes to put her in the car, despite her resistance. An ivory-colored Mercedes. I can still recall well how the car looked with its doors wide open. Your father was standing here, near the stone wall. He was wearing a black suit with a red tie. He had one foot in the house and one outside it, ready to intervene if need be. I don't know why he didn't take her himself or act more compassionately toward her. Then he called a meeting with all of us—servants, drivers, and guards—and warned us against saying where Mathilde had gone."

My father spread word around the village that he had sent Mathilde to stay with relatives on my mom's side of the family in the South, fearing as he did the intensification of the fighting here. But everyone had already heard that she had been taking drugs.

One day more than a year after her disappearance, Mathilde came back home, her hair cut short. She was still sad and her skin was still sallow.

My father was preparing to announce her engagement to my cousin George. She had come back against her will, as if compelled to atone for her sins for as long as she lived, as if they had stripped her of her beauty and put a curse on her that would follow her for the rest of her life.

My position in the house changed even after Mathilde came back. I had become the spoiled daughter of whom her father could deny no request. I was "Bella" to him. But this love of his carried the unspoken condition that I would keep far away from my sister.

I saw this in his eyes. My show of contempt for Mathilde was little different than anyone else's, but for me it was a lucrative means of getting toys, sweets, and other gifts. I started seeing Mathilde as another kind of fairy tale character—the heroine cast into the ovens of hell and whom no one could go near, or the witch forced to live in an abandoned cottage in the forest.

She seemed not to love me anymore. When my father wasn't there, I used to try to go to her and she would push me away. Once, though, she was really sad and asked me to come, and she hugged me tight. She started squeezing me hard, bursting into tears.

What did Mathilde want me to do? I ran away. I ran away from her and went to my father, terrified. Not that I was afraid of her. I loved her. I was afraid of the idea of disobeying my father's implicit instructions by getting near the witch. I can't describe how harsh this feeling was, nor why I acted like I did. I was a girl who didn't want to lose her feeling of security.

Now that I have come back home, I have started to see differently the throne I was sitting on. I want to ask Mathilde to let me hug her tight. You'll laugh I tell you that I can still see an ivory-colored Mercedes parked in front of the house. No, it isn't there, not really, but I still see it anyway.

When, after my return, my father started calling me by my pet name, "Bella," and telling me I hadn't changed, I wanted to tell him that I had changed more than he could possibly imagine. I wanted to tell him that Bella was really more like a dog's name, and I wasn't a dog.

You should know that I hugged my sister's children tight. I brought them lots of gifts from New York and I bought my sister a belt that matched the color of her eyes. When I went over to her to give her my gift, she took it without hugging me. "Why did you trouble yourself?" she asked me. I went closer to her and she stepped backward with her left foot, smiling as if giving a subtle sign to keep me away.

I understood. I reached out across the distance she imposed between us and touched her earring. "I just wanted to see what kind of stone you had in your earrings," I said as if justifying my desire to take her in my arms.

"Ruby. It's a ruby."

I was about to say that it was a beautiful stone when I felt my father's arms encircle me from far away. "Bella, come with me." He didn't let me agree before walking me outside. He started talking about village araq and kibbeh nayyeh. "Do you remember how I used to feed you kibbeh nayyeh, rolling it into little balls? Those were good times."

He put his arms around my waist and we walked in the garden, him talking: "You always played here.... There were so many things we did together. I want to take you around the village; there are a lot of people we should visit."

He spoke without waiting for my replies. Some of his questions were interspersed with excessive enthusiasm, pulling me to him from time to time and kissing my forehead. "You've always been my favorite daughter, and now look where you've gotten—Broadway. You will dance on Broadway, right? You will carry my name far and wide. You are the best young woman ever."

Anyone listening to my father talking would have been jealous of such a great love. But for me, these high expectations were a burden. My father knew nothing about my art and hadn't seen me dance even once, as if he had no ability to conceive of me outside the framework of home.

When I tried to speak or object to something he'd said, his face would suddenly go red and blaze with anger. "I didn't know that a girl like you could ask such questions. I actually can't believe it." Him saying this was enough to shut me up and make me stop talking altogether.

In childhood and adolescence, I was afraid of answering or asking questions. What my father said always seemed unquestionable, as if it descended from the heavens. But now when he's speaking, I get bored. At times I don't hesitate to show my restlessness while he's talking, as if I have returned to undo my previous passivity.

Losing my admiration for my father is very difficult, not only socially but even as my own internal decision. For many years I believed that the comfort I enjoyed was a sort of extra love. But isn't love supposed to let others be as they are? His way of interacting with my sister caused a rift between us that I couldn't just ignore when I grew up.

Before I went abroad, I tried many times to ask him to stop dealing with Mathilde with such contempt, to stop punishing her. Wasn't it he who had allowed Edouard into our house? Wasn't he part of this tragedy? He used to say that she had tricked him. He married her off to our relative to stop the scandal and to keep her under his control. My cousin, also now my sister's husband, was totally dominated by my father. "Go do this, son-in-law." "Come over here, son-in-law." The son-in-law never protested. He never said a thing.

The son-in-law worked for my father. He lived in the big, family house. He was one of us, the generation of children it is impossible to tell the difference between. All of these cousins have the same face. Mathilde wanted to regain our father's approval. She did what she could to be accepted again; she even named her firstborn son Asaad, after my father. The big Asaad embraced the little Asaad and took him on hunting trips "to make a man of him," as he used to say. But my sister's life stopped there: her attempts to gain my father's approval didn't improve their dealings with each other and her continued unhappiness.

I doubt she even wanted her son to go on these hunting trips and learn to shoot a gun at such a young age, but if this was what she had to offer as a sacrifice to her father, that's what it would be.

We would all gather around the table for lunch: Uncle George and his children, my sister and her family, my brother, his wife and kids, and me. Laurice would prepare all kinds of foods that I loved in my childhood. My father lifted his glass of araq every other second, shouting, "To Hilda's health, to the health of New York!" Everyone would mimic him. They raised glass after glass.

"To Hilda's health!" everyone would repeat. My father lowered his glass, and the other glasses would gradually be lowered to take their places on the table. I don't know if these good wishes really came from deep in the hearts of everyone in the group, especially from my sister, who was speaking in a mechanical, theatrical voice, like in a soap opera.

My father ate while talking about the village araq that Abu Moussa makes, about the Karakeh evening when the people of the village gather in his house and get together around the machine that extracts this araq which he used to distill, as if this atmosphere were necessary for the drink to have a local or homemade flavor. "Abu Moussa's araqs taste like they came straight from the vine. You don't taste the alcohol.... It's very important for the araq to be pure."

All nodded their heads as a sign they agreed with what my father said. He smiled. He lifted his glass again. "To Abu Moussa!" "To Abu Moussa," everyone repeated. The glasses returned to their places.

All went back to their plates once again, waiting for a new observation from my father.

"Don't you like our food anymore?" my father asked me directly once. "Why aren't you eating? Has your taste been spoiled by New York fast food?"

I smiled and stirred my soup with a spoon.

"Eat, Bella, eat. This feast is all in your honor."

The entire time, I asked myself, "Why did you come back?" I even started relying on English words when I found it difficult to express myself in Arabic. Some people were critical of me, as if I were doing it intentionally, but I had lived far away for more than six years. I wasn't the same Hilda who had left this place. And I had turned from a young girl into a woman.

I used to see this woman when I looked in the mirror, when you were flirting with me.

Why did I come back? Did I come back to get revenge on my father? To settle scores with him? To demand a late apology for my sister? Was I really the guilty one when it came to her? Why couldn't I stroll through the garden with her, the two of us talking like adults? Did I come back to see how we were all similar? Did I come back to revive my suffering and live it? Why do they seem like strangers to me? My God, how can faces weigh you down so much and be even harsher than memories?

Among all of them, only Laurice looked at me empathetically, as if she totally understood what was going on in my mind. There is something different when it comes to people who you've lived with since childhood, but who aren't your family or relatives. They feel differently about you; they don't expect anything from you. You aren't a part of them or an extension of them, so they try to see you as you are, not according to what they want themselves.

I was a child only to Laurice, because she alone could discover what I was seeing and know what was going on inside of me. Since childhood, she had known everything, the secrets of the house—where my father hid his weapons, where my mother hid her jewelry, the age of the flowers in the garden, our family disputes, the news of all the people in the village. She was like a lock box of events, an unpublished history and a sharp eye that nothing gets past.

I was able to be my natural self only in front of the two of them—Laurice and Giorgio. Together we could laugh like children. When Giorgio picked flowers and threw them at me and I did the same back, we collapsed in hysterical laughter as if we had become either mad or sensible. I used to love to laugh and play, to immerse myself in silliness, far from all my questioning of my roots.

It was never a matter of me hating the village. I really love it. I love its soil, its sky, its rockiness. Were it not for my contact with this land, I would never have felt life's beauty. My mother used to get angry when I came back with dirty clothes when I was young, asking Laurice to take me inside to wash.

"Mama can you tell me a story before I go to sleep?"

"Not today, darling, I'm tired."

"Mama, please!"

"Alright.... Once upon a time, a long time ago, there lived a little princess called Hilda."

"Did she have long hair?"

"Yes, long all the way down her back."

"Like Mathilde's hair?"

"Like Mathilde's hair."

"Mama, when will my sister come back?"

"Don't ask so many questions, little one, don't ask so many questions.... Pretty girls don't ask so many questions."

"But Mama ..."

"Come on, we are going to recite the Our Father and you are going to fall into a deep sleep."

"But Mama ..."

"Our Father, who art in heaven, hallowed be thy name...."

"Does our Father look like my dad?"

"Oh, Hilda, what are all these questions? Say your prayers quietly and go to sleep."

Whenever I prayed I used to close my eyes and squeeze my eyelids shut, as if this would make me more reverent. Sometimes I used to pray in a very loud voice, kneeling in front of the mirror and closing my eyes, hoping that my father and mother would hear me and come to pat me on the shoulder. "Deliver us from evil.... Thy will be done...." I raised my voice, making Laurice laugh.

What happened to the girl who used to run to her parents' laps? What happened to the girl who used to draw pictures of her little family, her in-between her mother and father? What happened to me? Why did I come back? To exhume the dead from their graves? Why can't I just leave things as they are? My father says toasts. My sister stays miserable. My mother continues her social climbing. We hardly see my brother, who runs my father's business and is picking up the scattered pieces of what remains of the party. We commemorate the yearly anniversary of my uncle, who committed suicide. And so on. Why don't these scenes satisfy me?

"Mom, come and look at my picture. This is me, this is Dad, and you are here, holding the ball because I'm tired. These are my cousins."

"What's this in the sky?"

"Those are the eyes of Uncle Freddy and his little daughter. They are with the Virgin Mary looking down at us."

"Oh, my little girl."

"Mom, will Uncle Freddy come back?"

"No...."

"Where is his wife?"

"She went back to her own town."

"Why didn't she stay here with us?"

No answer. No answer from my mother to any of my questions. I don't know why I had more questions when I spoke to my mother, why I rounded them off when talking to my father. The picture of Uncle Freddy, with his thick glasses, hung alone in the living room, a tangible memory of him. This was in addition to the yearly anniversary of his death that his wife didn't attend.

As I grew up, I had more questions. My mother kept refusing to give me answers and I kept hearing whispers here and there. Uncle Freddy had committed suicide after opening fire on three Palestinian fighters. He came home and killed himself afterward. His wife disappeared from the scene completely, exactly as my sister Mathilde did at a certain point.

When the war calmed a bit, my father enrolled me

in a dance school in Jounieh. I had taken some ballet classes when I was young, but had stopped because of the bombardments. Mathilde had also taken classes, but that suddenly vanished from her body and even her memory.

I got into the habit of dancing for my father on getting home from the school. He would call Uncle George to come watch also, and he clapped loudly while my sister watched from a distance. For my father, it was a beautiful scene, but he never imagined that I would one day tell him I wanted to dance professionally.

Of course he didn't want to send me to New York, and I didn't have the finances to go there on my own.

I could have sworn that my father changed his mind only because he heard my sister agree with him.

"The girls in our family shouldn't travel alone, especially to dance. What will the people in the village say about us!"

"You, in particular, may not express your opinion on the matter. We have seen what girls in our family do when living under their father's roof. Hilda will travel abroad, despite them all!" This was his last word on the matter, and no one objected.

After he agreed, I promised to also enroll in fashion design courses, to assure that I had a practical specialization. "*Haute couture*," my mother shouted aloud. "*ça sera magnifique ma chérie!*" She was speaking French as if I were already working in one of the great French fashion design houses.

"Mama, I'm going to New York, not Paris."

"Ah, *les bijoux encore!* Imagine only the clothes and the ..."

"Mama, I want to dance."

"You will make the most beautiful dresses. Don't forget your mom."

She was enthusiastic about something that might never happen. I only smiled, deciding to let her be happy.

My father sent me an allowance every month and showered me with money. When I spoke to him from New York and told him that I had started to sort myself out, that I could get money by working with a fashion design firm, and that I had joined a dance group alongside my studies, his anger flared.

"I am the one who will support you even if you are at the ends of the earth."

His financial support was coupled with the ritual of talking to him by phone every morning and evening to report the details of my day. My mother would interrupt him: "Bella, where are the dresses?"

It was good in the beginning but slowly turned into a burden.

"I want you to come back to us."

"But, Dad, I can't do that."

"People are starting to gossip here. You have one month to come back or I will be angry with you."

"You can't just ask me to come back, not now; I just started my journey … my future. …"

I wasn't able to finish: my father hung up on me after I heard my mother saying, "Assad, the dresses."

You and I were just getting to know each other back then. I didn't tell you about my relationship with my family during our first dates. I wanted you to see me as just Hilda.

Of course I didn't agree to go back. My father cut off my allowance for two months, and when he felt that this wouldn't work, he went back to calling me every morning, speaking in a soft tone.

"I will support you until I die. You have to think about coming back, Hilda. Don't stay away for so long, my girl."

Whenever I was more stubborn and insisted on staying away, his voice would get calmer. Why did my father act so weak in front of me, and why did I like this? He started sending unprecedented amounts of money, taking on the role of being the supporter of my ambitions.

From far away I discovered that I resented my father.

Back home I had lived a constrained life, one befitting a girl I didn't want to be. I would tremble in fear if I disobeyed my father's orders, if I acted against his instructions, if I wore a dress he disliked, if I went near my sister, if I asked questions, if I didn't pray.

One way or another, my presence in New York made me immune to him. I used to return for very short visits. By explaining how busy I was in America, I didn't have to spend a long time back in Lebanon. But for the past three last years I stopped visiting altogether, because I really was busy with work. I didn't notice how much I'd changed, and it didn't occur to me that seven years living far away would be so formative an experience.

When I came back here, I used to act mockingly toward my father, in stark contrast with the shyness I would have shown around him before. I would laugh aloud, bring Giorgio to the house, and play with my brother and sister's children, teaching them silly things, such as making irritating noises with their hands, or messing with my mother's antiques in the sitting room.

All of these naughty childish behaviors weren't appropriate for my age, but I used to enjoy them so much that I once even invited Mathilde to play with us when we were in the garden.

I whispered in her son's ear to go and beg her to come even if he had to go and pull her dress.

When she came, all the children were begging her in unison to sit with us.

"Mathilde, Mommy Mathilde, Auntie Mathilde," they all started chanting.

She crossed one leg over the other and sat down. The children all started trying to teach her how to make that irritating sound: "You put your hand like this.... No, no! Put your thumbs here, now blow." They all started to clap for her when she made the sound. She smiled for a while and then laughed. Her laughter seemed as if it were coming alive for the first time, a forgotten laugh. Her eyes watered and she almost cried. A long time ago she used to cry often, but beautiful tears with a laugh and smile.

"Yes, sister," she now said.

I stepped over to her and embraced her and we cried and then laughed together. Telling her I loved her a lot, I started running my fingers through her hair as if I were trying to bring it back, as if combing it a bit would make it grow again.

I remembered my years spent in foreign countries, when I had almost completely cut off all ties with my sister except for short telephone calls. The strange thing is that, then, I didn't feel this nostalgia, which the distance traveled determines. I wasn't a spoiled, delicate girl afraid of living in places she didn't know. A few times I felt sad and lonely, but for fleeting moments that I would recover from quickly, as if I had totally forgotten I wasn't from here.

I think we sort of overexaggerate how we cherish the homeland in our descriptions of it. I know that you, for example, describe Palestine numerous times every day, in your imagination, but my land was significant in all its disappointments and memories of its wars.

I wanted to liberate myself from the concept of the first house and not belonging there. I used to be eager to see the places where Martha Graham danced. I devoured everything in the city ferociously, the narrow streets, the crowds, as if I were living in an Atari or PlayStation video game.

I found that I didn't really love everything I had loved previously—not the big table we gathered around every day, not the extended visits to friends and relatives. My previous life seemed—if we excluded dance from it—merely a big waste of time.

I even loved getting to know boys in New York before I met you. I lost my virginity in the back seat of a car belonging to a man I met there. He didn't believe me when I told him I was a virgin. He started laughing: "A virgin at 24? Are you joking?"

I screamed when he penetrated me and then he knew I wasn't joking. "My God, you are actually a virgin."

He didn't stop. He did it. I went back to my apartment as if I didn't believe I was no longer a virgin. I wasn't happy or sad. I was merely stunned as if suddenly

I had a body. When I would go back to the village for a short holiday, I felt I had a secret that no one knew.

While on the phone my mother often tried to lure me into revealing if I had a relationship with a man. I would answer her slyly. "Why are you asking so many questions, Mama?" Then I would tell her that I was busy and didn't have time for such things.

"I'm in New York, Mom, there are no virgins in the city," I would say with a laugh after hanging up the phone.

Perhaps sometimes I was a little evil, more than I should have been. Seditious, I loved stirring up trouble by mocking my father's convictions. Maybe I was also blunt and rude or even provocative. But it was too late to ever again go back and become the Hilda they'd made. Women are like this: when they lose the innocence attributed to them, nothing will bring it back.

I don't know how I ever rid myself of my guilt. Perhaps the Patricia incident in my childhood had taught me to question the nuns—that and the act of contrition I had been saying since childhood but without guilt. It took discipline to keep from drifting into the past or regretting having broken with my family's expectations of me. But I didn't care if I lost or won. I was living my passion—my passion for dance, life, and art.

But in my lack of belonging, had I really won? If I had, why did I have to return? I remember how many times you asked me to trust our love alone, but I found myself unable to. I wasn't so sure whether love is fundamentally about belonging or limitations. I didn't know why I should see you as a homeland. I made our bed and folded your clothes with love, like wives do, but I didn't know if I was doing this to create a new household or not.

I was torn away from my first home. I clean the windows in this absurd second home, and I laugh aloud as if it's a game. I fall into your lap in the sky, and I give myself to you, completely covering you. I used to wake up and feel your warmth next to me. This warmth sometimes stayed with me all day long, as if I hid a little piece of the sun in my heart. But sometimes an image of my first place would come to me—a memory—as if it were challenging me with not being able to make new memories in its place. Did you see me returning to look at it and tell it that I could? Perhaps I also came back to occupy this memory, to tell it that we can arrive at some kind of settlement: to expand into all places and be done with our enmity toward our roots.

-2-

That morning, when I went with Laurice to visit Giorgio, I pressured her the whole way to tell me why my uncle's wife was no longer a part of our family.

"Your father kicked her out because he held her responsible for his brother's death."

"What did she do wrong?"

"Why are you insisting on bringing back all these memories?"

"What was he like? Tell me about him."

"He was very intelligent and handsome but he had a bad temper."

"Yes, what else?"

"He used to beat her."

"He beat his wife?"

"Yes, he beat Amaal."

"Why?"

"Listen, Hilda. Her skin would be black and blue from the beatings."

"Didn't he love her?"

"He loved her madly, but he had sexual problems. He could seldom do what he needed to do in bed ... and then he would beat her."

"My God, what bullshit."

"Amaal is a beautiful and refined woman. Your uncle didn't kill anyone. The Palestinians arrested him once and confiscated his weapon. Yes, he was missing for several nights. Your father mediated with his kidnappers. He paid a big ransom. Your uncle came back broken. He didn't speak for days because of the torture. He took tranquilizers for his nerves but his crisis got worse. He wanted to kill Amaal.... He accused her of betraying him. But he couldn't kill her. He pointed his gun at her and she was crying and terrified but then he emptied it into his own head."

"What are you saying? He didn't kill them?"

"No, your father wanted to make his suicide a heroic act. It was a tragedy!"

Anger took hold inside me, a fire that was suddenly ignited, a fire I could no longer extinguish. So this story had also been a lie. Majd also shared my uncle's tragedy. We killed his mother, and they insulted and tortured my uncle. We both committed crimes. No not us, Majd and me. We didn't kill anyone. Surely anger is what pushes me myself, and him too, to carry around what happened long before. We love each other. So we won't hurt each other like that. For my father, isn't this part of his building up the war like heroism, the denial of any defeat?

"Those Palestinians, why did they arrest him? What did he do to them? What did his wife do wrong? Was she cheating on him?"

"No, dear, no. I know her. I won't lie. Christ commands us not to lie. It was a fantasy of his. Everything was in his head."

"Laurice, but my father, my father said ..."

"Your father wanted to preserve his dignity, their dignity."

"But he lied to me."

"No, no.... Our master doesn't lie. It is not a lie. He wanted to protect the family from people's gossip. You know how people talk, Hilda. The master is a good man, a strong man. The reason he said your uncle killed them was to keep from being broken himself."

"The Palestinians.... Laurice, who are the Palestinians?"

"What is this question?"

"Are they really the enemy? Did we have to kill them and they kill us?"

"They ..."

"Laurice, I need to know who they are.... Did they really destroy our country?"

"Hilda, I don't know. I'm just a maid."

"Oh, Laurice, the sounds of bombardment, all those wars, all that death, everything was terrible."

"I know."

"Sometimes everything seems like there's no end—guards outside the house, Mathilde's sadness, a gun collection in the house. Everything is terrible. We woke up suddenly to see the war had stopped, but its scent lingers here, still as fresh and viscous as blood, like a wound that won't heal."

We kept walking with Laurice muttering, "Virgin Mary, Mother Mary, oh Mary, Holy Mary, Virgin Mary." I held her hand as if seeking out security or calm, as if we were both part of the story and could empathize with each other ... to bond together. There's a bond between people that's stronger than words—what you feel when you put your hand in theirs, what happens to you when you look in their eyes and you know their stories. What can't be summarized by talking is the essence of human relationships.

I wanted to tell her that I was in love with you, a Palestinian, but whenever I started to move my tongue, it betrayed me. Finally, I gathered up my courage and shouted in a loud voice, "Laurice, I'm in love with a Palestinian guy. I'm in love with a Palestinian man, Laurice." I said it just like that, as if the words were racing to all come out at once. My hand slipped away and she looked at me, shouting back, "You're mad."

"I am mad, Laurice.... Yes I'm crazy, but crazy in a good way. Like Giorgio. Madness isn't necessarily bad."

"Oh, my dear, of all the men on the face of the earth ..."

"It's love, Laurice. Love doesn't choose according to social conventions."

She smiled, and I looked at the woman who had cared for me and my siblings in our childhood. The woman who had washed our clothes, ironed our shirts, and made our beds. She was short. Her black hair hung to her shoulders. She wasn't beautiful according to typical standards of feminine beauty but she was good-hearted and kind. She had never married, had children, or ever dreamed of leaving my father's house, which was my grandfather's when Laurice had come here as a servant at the age of thirteen.

Her mother died young and her father sent her to work for my family in order to relieve himself of the burden of raising her. She wasn't unhappy. She was satisfied, as if she didn't know any other possibilities existed. "You're a dignified and generous family," her father had said when he brought her. "Don't worry, she's in good hands," my grandmother had answered him. Then she took Laurice and asked her to wash up, gave her new clothes, and started teaching her about everything in the house—how to get along with my uncles and how the house was run. My grandmother taught her the golden rule: What happens between these walls stays between these walls.

Laurice had witnessed every important thing that happened in the family: she knew all the little details and memorized them. Even my grandmother would ask her again and again if she wanted to be free, to marry, to have a life outside of our house. "I want to leave the house to go to the cemetery, ma'am. I don't want anything else." She didn't say this with sorrow or sadness, but with the complete conviction of a pious woman who saw our house as something like a temple.

During the war, Laurice would clean the floors of the house after the wounded came, always finishing by spraying water over the threshold to expel the demons. She didn't minister to the fighters, because her fragility would have made her collapse. This was the opposite of my mother, who transformed in some situations into a solid woman—different from the pampered one we were used to.

My mother had the ability to see blood and deal with it. Relief for the wounded was a serious matter to her. There was no time for alarm or panic. She would take out alcohol and cotton and ask Laurice to bring hot water and bandages. She did her job fully and then would go to bed extremely exhausted and fall asleep as if something normal had just ended, as if blood had become a part of our daily lives.

-3-

Uncle George used to spend most of his time in a small underground cellar made up of three rooms, two of which were connected by an archway. We children weren't allowed to enter this place and for a long time I thought it was like the depths of hell. According to my mother, he was the only one with the key. I knew that one of the rooms was used as the household's pantry to store vats of olive oil, lentils, and wine.

In the beginning of each autumn, the Arab migrant workers—as my father used to call them—came to harvest the olives before my family sent them to the press. Their womenfolk came too and spread plastic mats down on the ground where they sat pressing the olives close together before packing them into glass jars with lemon and oil.

They covered their heads and spoke a lot while working. I wasn't allowed to mix with them much, for fear of "lice," according to my mother. Their hands were black at the end of the day, and rough from long periods of toil.

The village elders brought in these Arab migrant workers to live in tents or cement houses with tin roofs during the olive harvest season. I used to enjoy the bustle in the village, and at home it meant I finally saw some movement after the war ended.

The secret of the first room was known therefore, but the other two rooms next to it remained a mystery to me. When I returned this time, I insisted on accompanying Uncle George to his headquarters down in the cellar. Faced with my relentless, insistent nagging, he agreed.

We descended the stairway slowly and stood in front of the cellar for a few minutes.

"Listen, Hilda, you know your uncle George only as an uncle."

"I know lots of things."

"What do you know?"

"That you and my father were fighters."

"Your father was a leader, not an ordinary fighter."

"You know that I used to see you two carrying weapons and guns and going out at night.... I used to see many people gathering in the living room. Uncle, I've grown up. I'm not a little girl anymore."

"Those days ..."

"What about those days? Were they good days?"

"We were strong, we believed that we would never be defeated. Our dream, our greater Lebanon."

"And what's left of all that now?"

"We were going to rule this country, build up its glory."

"With war?"

"War, ferocity, sometimes all of this is necessary."

I cut him off and told him, "Uncle, open the door and let's continue the conversation inside." I was afraid that he was having second thoughts and would ask me to rethink the idea of entering his secret room. He put the key in the lock. He moved it to the right. "Toq!" he turned the first lock, "toq!" he turned the second one. I heard the creak of the wooden door, which he deliberately pushed inward so we could enter.

He reached out toward the door and pushed a button to turn on the light. A yellow bulb cast a shadow over the room and I stood nailed to my place. I wasn't in the cellar. I was in an artist's atelier. The two connected rooms were divided by an arch. One of them contained statues and sculptures and the other raw materials—clay, stone, chisels, and molds.

"What is this? Who made all this?"

"Your uncle George."

"Why do you hide it all?"

I walked around the room looking at the sculptures. Most of them were people with missing body parts. A man with no fingers. Another without ears. A woman whose breasts were cut off and with another woman lying across her belly. Statues of men without legs or without heads. A statue of artillery. Other sculptures were body parts: a hand, an ear, a leg.

He started pointing to the sculptures. "I made some of them out of rock and stone, carved with a chisel; others are made of metal. Look, this one is made of clay; I made it with my hands and then put it in a plaster mold to take this shape."

"Why did you make it like that?"

"Like what?"

"Missing something."

I didn't know if this was art and if I should show that I was amazed by these sculptures. I didn't even know if he wanted to invoke amazement. I thought we lived in a big house that had dead bodies or human rubble beneath it. This place was like a curse, this nation was like a collective cemetery in which everyone is buried and then they build homes atop it. In our cellar, I came face to face with victims of bombardments and also the artillery fire that my uncle couldn't get out of his mind. There was no spattering of bright red blood but I swear I could almost hear human howls and groans.

Why are memories so painful when they are awoken inside a person? Why can't we look straight at the past and say calmly, "That was in the past"? Why isn't pain something fleeting and ordinary? Why do we cry again when certain images come to us, and why, once this memory returns, is it impossible to laugh or remember a nice or funny time? What is the secret that sadness carries and makes it so resistant to fading away?

My uncle's voice interrupted me while I was lost in those moments. He put his hand on my shoulder and asked, "Why did you come back here, Hilda?"

Why did I come back? I asked myself once again, staring at the sculptures. I tried to resist the tears flooding my eyes and gather together some courage to tell him, "I came back here precisely because if I hadn't looked right at all this loss I wouldn't be able to go forward."

"But you abandoned everything completely and were so distant from us, and then all of a sudden you came back wanting simply to hold us accountable. You are prejudiced against us."

"I came back to see you, to see my mother and sister and ..."

"And who, Hilda? You came back to drag a confession out of your father, to make all of us confess. I see it in your eyes, your questions and your condemnation. You want to know how many people we killed? You want us to count up the dead bodies for you? Will that help you? My family are war criminals? You'll go back to New York and complain about your family's injustice? What do you want? We are your flesh and blood, my girl. If you strip us off you, it will hurt only you, not us."

"I just want to understand. That's all there is to it."

"You are just exhausting yourself, that's it. You won't ever convince anyone to go back on their decisions, my niece."

"Uncle, your sculptures reveal your guilt."

He burst out in laughter so loud it filled every corner of the cellar.

"Guilt? My sculptures reveal life, powerfully. We were powerful. Nothing could break our arms."

"Broken limbs.... What power?"

"The power that kept this house standing, the power that gave you the opportunity to go abroad and study dance, to live in luxury and comfort. They took everything from us, don't you understand? Everything. We had to fight and kill to protect what was ours."

"What are you doing now? Did you win?"

"We tried."

"Is this victory? The ruin of humanity? Do you know, Uncle, that what is most painful about the war is that most people died terrified, deprived of even lying on their sickbeds, smiling, and peacefully saying that their souls should rest in peace."

"Should I sculpt a sun and flowers to satisfy you, Hilda? Should I paint you a tree? This is life, my girl. I don't want to be hard on you, but it really doesn't help for you to come here and lay all this blame on us."

"Uncle, I don't want a tree. I grew up in the time of trees."

"Shall we go back upstairs?"

"Yes, let's go upstairs."

-4-

Most people here think it's easy to throw yourself into the unknown, to decide to pack your life in a suitcase and just leave. Even I don't know how I was able to do it. They laugh when I speak English and ask me to speak more slowly. They don't know that I've changed. They try to cancel out the seven years I've lived far away from them or abbreviate them into one request: "Tell us about America."

My sister laughs and puts her hand over her mouth. I started making up stories, saying that women there have four eyes and men have no teeth. I resorted to sarcasm. My brother, looking all well-put-together, interrupted me, telling my father about industry over there, as well as progress, capital, and companies. My father nods his head proudly. I put up with their interruptions, say something about New York, and then am silent.

Do you know why? I found I didn't know this city that I had lived in for seven years. I could say that it is an enchanting place, but I couldn't tell them that I really knew it. Then the conversation changes. I ask my sister to go out on the balcony with me for a bit. My father looks at me and is not pleased. I take her hand and we go out.

"You know Mathilde, the best thing about New York is that I am a stranger there. I don't want to know that city well; I don't want to make new memories. I only enjoy being a stranger."

"But you'll need new memories some day."

"No.... Why burden myself?"

"But you returned here because you needed these memories."

"No, I returned for you all ... to see you all. You, for example, wouldn't you prefer to live somewhere else?"

"Not at all."

"But you aren't happy here."

"We are all doing well, we're happy, especially now that the war's ended."

"Sister, what happiness is this? I hardly ever see you laugh."

"I have a family: my children, Mom and Dad, and my husband."

"Dad? Aren't you upset with our dad?"

"Why would I be?"

"He oppressed you, Mathilde, don't you feel that?"

"You can't talk about him in that way. Our father is a great man."

"But Mathilde ..."

"Listen, Hilda, I made a mistake, I have to take responsibility for my actions. I want to repent for my sins. Hopefully he'll forgive me one day."

I didn't want to believe what I was hearing. My sister with her long hair thinks that she's nothing but a sinner. She started telling me for the first time about the period when she was lost and describing her feelings of euphoria that preceded her coma. "God save us," she repeated between sentences.

As I listened to her I found myself feeling that confessing sins wasn't a virtue in all cases but a kind of surrender. Whenever I tried to interrupt her to remind her that my father himself used to provide the fighters with drugs during the war, her skin would flush and she would take up his defense. She would justify it by saying that he was preparing them better to fight. I listened to her and realized that I had killed my father and with him killed parts of myself. I had killed the imaginary homeland by sitting on it. These offences and what came after amounted to an extreme betrayal, and I experienced the euphoria that came with it. I picked up soil and dust and rubbed them on my face, chest, and the rest of my body. Then I returned to what had once been my home to take pleasure in having killed and wrapped the victims in shrouds, after which I buried them with my own hands and started crying like criminals who've committed their crimes unintentionally.

Next I danced on their graves, the dance of a woman tearing her body away from it all. They were under me, under the rhythmic beating of my feet, and yet they did not move. Spectators were applauding. They didn't see what was buried under this theater. They saw only a body coming out of a body, multiplying, and they believed that it was a wonderful scene.

I listened to Mathilde with surprise and asked myself if I was the only one who saw the problems here. Why don't they object to everything that we went through? Why can my father clone everyone in his own image?

I wanted to show them mirrors so they might see the cracks in their souls, *our* souls, but they were calm to the point of exasperation, like boulders impossible to move. Whenever I looked at them I blamed myself for my curiosity. Sometimes I really envied their blindness.

Martha Graham said, "No artist is pleased. There is no satisfaction whatever at any time. There is only a queer, divine dissatisfaction, a blessed unrest that keeps us marching and makes us more alive than the others."

Perhaps she was right, but she forgot to say that this cursed unrest makes us descend to the lowest of the low, forcing us to dance with demons even as it allows us to be called professional dancers. Perhaps I was condemned to this unrest in order to create my art, to force my body to be reborn.

-5-

The sun rose early this morning. I stood contemplating its rays. Is this light that oversees each and every day ever-present, or is it continually reborn, making it possible for new colors to emerge? I was thinking about how memories change, how we return to distant villages and there see the men we used to flirt with carrying their children in their arms. How does the man I danced with for the first time see me now that I have grown up and dyed my hair? How did the trees we exchanged kisses under become simply a part of nature? How does a woman forget the man who gave her her first kiss? How does she know that he hasn't become another man? How does she know that she isn't another woman? How do the wheels of time stop, and yet why can we never go back to what we were?

I also used to think of you, how you used to tell me that America was dangerous and that New York was like a hell that a person could only want to escape from. "There is a vast difference between the American people and their government.... The American and Israeli governments deny our civilizations, throw our monuments away, murder us, disperse our families, and then tell the world that we are criminals. America is a dangerous country, because it takes an inventory of its own real injustice and creates another kind of fake injustice, which is merely an excuse for covering up power. The story is lost, my dear, and we are lost with it."

War stories are all the same. The fighter finds an excuse to cover up his crimes, and the oppressed person finds a justification to burden himself with guilt. The truth is lost between distorted interests, and no one is left to tell it or even to listen to it. Everyone here is saying that they had to fight. They see ferocity as relative, as a necessary reaction to circumstances imposed upon them. My father is therefore a sinless, infallible hero to them.

I tried to call you a while ago but you were really hard on me. I swore that I wouldn't speak to you again and I thought perhaps you would understand some day. Today in particular being away from you is hard, as if there were a hole in my womb that only you could fill.

I needed to speak to you to feel that another Hilda is still there somewhere. I look at myself and feel that I am a different woman.

All the places back here formed a fundamental part of my being. And then there were the scents I smelled for so many years. The nests of the birds I used to watch. The people in the village. Everything. There was a huge gap between me and them. It was as if I never knew them, as if this girl whom everyone loved and played with was no longer me.

Today I spotted Giorgio from the balcony. He was running to escape some children. I rushed toward them. He had fallen. His leg was cut. As soon as the children saw me approaching they ran far away. I cursed them and threatened to punish them. Giorgio's face was red; he was spewing angrily, like a dragon. He was ripping grass out of the ground and throwing it behind himself.

"Giorgio, you're bleeding. Come with me so we can treat your wound."

"Aaaah aaaah," he said, starting to shake his head.

"You have to come with me, Giorgio. I am begging you. Listen to me this one time only."

He wouldn't agree. I ran home quickly and brought disinfectant, towels, and bandages for his cut. He was sitting in the same position, still pulling grass up out of the ground. I extended his leg and started cleaning the wound. He pulled his leg back. I got him to stretch it back out.

"Dogs.... I will find them; they really hurt you."

I kept talking to him as I wiped the blood from his foot. When I lifted my eyes to look at Giorgio, I saw him crying silently, bitterly.

"Oh, habibi, don't cry like that. What's wrong, Giorgio?"

I came closer to him and took him in my arms.

"My dear, you wanted to have a mother to make you breakfast and wait for you when you came home from school. You wanted to be a normal boy like them, didn't you?"

He was a child trapped in a man's body. He continued groaning, and we stayed sitting there for nearly half an hour before he stood up again. We went in the house. My father was in the living room.

"Hilda, why do you insist on being with this madman?"

"Daddy!"

He kept speaking negatively, so I went into the kitchen and asked Laurice to take care of Giorgio and take him home. I went out angrily and asked him, "Why do you act like that toward him?"

"By God, he's crazy. Don't act like that and defend him."

"Listen, Daddy, maybe Giorgio used to be forbidden from coming in the house previously, but not now. Not when I'm here."

"This is my house and my rules go here."

"I'll leave it to you and then never come back. I swear to you."

"You ungrateful girl.... Everything I do is for you."

This was the first time I confronted my father directly. The entire family quickly gathered around us. I was insistent on keeping steady and seeming strong. Everyone started asking me to go to my room. When I felt ready to collapse, that's what I did. I shot him a defiant glance and went up to my room. I closed the door and burst into tears. My mother followed me, "Hilda open the door." I didn't answer. "Hilda, honey, what's wrong? Open the door."

I opened it in response to her insistence. "Hilda why are you fighting with your father? Why are you crying? What's wrong, honey?"

"Why does he want to kick out Giorgio?"

She started telling me I should have grown out of all this silliness and was behaving inappropriately.

"Mom, my whole life you've asked me to love Jesus Christ. Mama, Christ loved the weak and the poor, and now you're blaming me because I feel compassion for an orphaned boy."

I could have continued on and narrated to her how our family violates religious teachings by simply asking for forgiveness day and night but doing nothing more. Instead I sunk into a feverish sobbing that I wouldn't have dared risk when I was young, when I too had held to the notion that tears were an offence we must go all out to avoid, even if circumstances did sometimes compel us to commit it.

I was crying for many reasons—among them, that this place seemed like utter loneliness, with no place for strangers. And I had become a stranger. All they know about me is that I specialize in fashion design and dance. Some implicitly consider me a brazen whore, but because of family considerations they don't express this opinion openly. But I know what is said in the tight little women's circles. "A girl who leaves here for America to wiggle her hips. She had to go all the way to America just to wiggle her hips?" I don't care that much about what they say even if it saddens me. But sometimes I have to cry to be sure I'm still alive. Somewhere inside me, I had go to overcome their expectations about me, like someone who throws herself into the fire, moving from flame to flame. This burning feeling became a kind of addiction, a search for some kind of truth, exactly like dance. Forcing the body again and again to push its limits, to create many bodies. When I danced, I used to address God to the beat of the music, a god they always used to force me to ask forgiveness from. I invited him to join in my earthly pleasures to become flesh and blood exactly like me.

6

Day after day my father's patience wore thin. He called my behavior juvenile, reckless, and inappropriate. I turned up my music and danced in my room. I went out for hours with Giorgio. I laughed really loudly. I also started not knowing what I was trying to prove to him, and what I was doing here. Whenever I looked at the walls surrounding me, I understood why I had left.

He would come into my room sometimes and pretend he wasn't upset with me. He would ask me to dance for him. I would do so. He would talk to me about the olive harvest. He reminded me how I used to play in his lap when I was a girl. But he didn't ask me what was wrong.

I looked at him and asked about the war again. Why had Uncle Freddy killed himself, why was his wife forbidden from visiting us? Father repeated the same narrative. He even grew increasingly obstinate. Some people deserved to die, he said, like the Palestinians whom, he claimed, my uncle had killed. He said many things and told me he had been promised an important position in the government and that the ministry he aspired to would bring us our victory.

He said that the party, while its influence was now on the decline, would no doubt return to its former glory. He said he'd visited "our Master" today, that influential cleric he knows. "Things will change for us, Hilda. Surely you feel the injustice and inequality today as much as I do, but things will be made right."

I told him that his assumptions about me were a mistake, that I hadn't left because we'd lost the war but indeed because we'd fought it in the first place. He laughed and patted my head, telling me I didn't mean what I was saying, because I was still young. He also told me that he would see to everything, including restoring the power and influence of the past.

There was only one voice in the room—his voice. I wanted to raise mine to tell him that whenever he spoke, something in the way he moved his mouth and in his insistence on playing the role of unsung hero, alienated from the world, made me feel that I was watching a long film on television. This mystery he tried to surround himself with in fact laid him bare before me. Even as he sought to make all this about himself recede in the distance, he couldn't see what was right in front of him. His tone was condescending, and yet he was aware of having been completely crushed: he lived within a total fallacy. I carefully observed this contradiction within him, and no matter how much he spoke to me, I could hear it only as a monologue rooted in a lifetime of delusions.

This was exactly what I and other members of the family had clung to our whole lives—delusions of power. That we were the best and the brightest. If my father told us that a Palestinian in the West wasn't returning his daughter's phone calls, what would we do? What if I had thrown myself on my father's mercy and told him that sometimes it seemed to me that you want to take revenge on me for what they had done to you, your people?

Would he understand if the roles were reversed? Would he understand that the drugs he'd given other people's children got to his daughter, that the wounds afflicting the victims' bodies found their way also into our hearts? What if I had told him that it's possible that he helped murder your family without knowing it? That I know why my uncle died? Would this stop him or simply make him angry and even harsher?

I decided to stay quiet, because confrontation wouldn't change either of our opinions. I knew, when I listened to his voice, alone in the room, that my suitcases were calling me to buy a new ticket, to return to the land of my dreams.

"Dad, I'm leaving tomorrow."

"What?"

"I'm leaving tomorrow, baba."

"Didn't you come back wanting to stay here with me, Hilda? You're like a stranger. After everything I tried to do for you, you want to go abroad again. How long will you be away this time?"

I didn't answer. I slammed the door violently and he repeated, "You're such an ungrateful little girl."

We were all gathered together around the dining room table. My suitcases were waiting in the living room, lined up next to each other, as if they were even more excited than me to leave.

Everyone was eating with unaccustomed calm. It seemed to be the first time there had been no sound in the house. I broke the silence by announcing that there was something important I wanted to say before I left. I started talking about you.

"I met a really great guy in New York. He has nice features and is very successful in his profession. We've spent a lot of time together without ever feeling bored. He's always treated me kindly. He held a mirror up to me and showed me reflections, colors I've never seen before, and warmed me up. He loves me a lot, too. Sometimes his behavior is childish but sometimes he looks out for me."

They all listened without any reaction. I carried on speaking, telling them that you, like me, were a stranger in New York and that we both needed to be strangers. I also told them that I loved your black eyes, and described how they shone in the dark. Then I told them that there was a scar on your face and that you couldn't walk very well.

"Why is he like this?" my sister asked. "Why haven't you told us about him before? Where is he? Why didn't he come here with you?"

"Oh, I forgot to mention that he's of Palestinian origin and that his injuries resulted from shrapnel that wounded him at Sabra and Shatila."

I had barely finished my sentence and put my fork down to get ready to go amid their astonishment when I heard knocking at the door. It was a delegation of people from the village. Women trilling. Men shooting rifles in the air. My brother entered, heralding the news: "Dad, Dad, your name appeared in the new cabinet reshuffle....

They're going to announce it this afternoon. I'm sure of it. Your Excellency the Minister, Minister of Social Affairs."

Your Excellency the Minister, Your Excellency the Minister.

Congratulations, congratulations. Joyful noise. Guns fired in the air. I took my suitcases calmly and withdrew from the hullabaloo. They didn't notice me in the crowds of well-wishers. The driver was waiting for me outside. I didn't look back. All that noise allowed me to justify my disappearance without making a fuss.

Translator's Acknowledgments

Like all translations, this one was a collective endeavor that benefitted from the labor and support of many people. My first thanks go to Jana Elhassan, who took the time to discuss her novel with me, read a draft, and offered her input. I would also like to acknowledge Michel Moushabeck of Interlink Publishing and the whole team there for their work and commitment to publishing Arabic literature in translation. It was again a pleasure to work with copyeditor Paul Olchváry, who immensely improved the translation. I would like to express sincere thanks to Katy Kalemkerian and Hadi Hoteit for their dedicated work helping me with the details of words and sentences, as well as discussions about the work. For this I would also like to acknowledge Nada Saab.

The translation was completed in Lebanon, and those people who afforded me space and time there are owed a thanks that brief words cannot express: Iman Humaydan, Yasmine Nachabe Taan and the Nachabe, Taan, Fakih, and Merhej families. For patience, support and conversations that helped, thanks also to Amanda Hartman, rosalind hampton, Aziz Choudry, and Tameem Hartman. The translation is dedicated to all of us who live and love across borders and through trauma.